THE RED LEDGER
part 1

MEREDITH WILD

THE **RED LEDGER**
part 1

MEREDITH WILD

WATERHOUSE PRESS

For Sean, my little writer

1

ISABEL

Rio de Janeiro

Carnaval saturates the streets like a thousand tiny rivers of excess and desire. Heat and music and the ebb and flow of revelers create an undeniable pulse of excitement. It exists in the balmy ocean air, settles on my skin, and sizzles against my nerve endings. I feel like I could drown in it.

"Do you want another drink?"

Kolt's American accent stands out in the cacophony of the open-air bar.

I don't need another drink. The alcohol from the few caipirinhas I've already had flows through my bloodstream, making me horny and impulsive. I meet his gaze and consider where I want the night to go.

"We have to work tomorrow." I'm not sure if that will discourage him, though.

"Then maybe we shouldn't waste all night here."

I smirk. "What are you trying to say?"

"I've been staring at you in that dress all night. And right now, I'm willing to do just about anything to have a couple hours alone with you."

With his soft brown eyes, he rakes me in, betraying his desire. He's smooth-shaven with lightly tanned skin. His short, dirty-blond hair has grown out just enough to curl naturally at the ends—as close to rugged as he'll ever look.

I swirl the ice in my glass. "A couple hours?"

He rests his hand on my lower back and presses his lips to my bare shoulder. "You know I want a lot more than that."

I tense. I care about Kolt. Deep down, I know he cares about me too. But every time I sleep with him, I feel his grip tighten on me as if I'm becoming more his. He doesn't understand I'm not his at all. I can't give him more.

But I can give him tonight. One more night.

"Let's go back to my place," I say, silently promising myself I'll indulge the physical attraction one last time.

His eyes widen a fraction before returning to normal. He gets the attention of the bartender with his broken Portuguese and pays him quickly. He makes no effort to fit in here. Most days he looks like he should be strolling the grounds at Harvard, the very place that shaped him through undergrad and another shaky year in grad school.

Kolt's on vacation from his life. It's been six months.

In another six, he'll go back to it, and I know as surely as I know my own name that he intends to bring me back with him. I tick off all the boxes. We have chemistry. If we both ignored my inability to love him, I could fit into his life nicely. He's rich and driven, and every time he looks at me, I know what he sees. A pretty fuck. A prize to be won. A match.

But I'm not on vacation. I'm running away. The urge to thrust myself into a future unknown was so powerful, it landed me in Rio. In the center of this chaos is exactly where I want to be—until I can find the truth. But the truth is like this overwhelming place. It's much easier to get lost than to ever find what you're looking for.

"Let's go." Kolt slips his hand into mine, and we're off.

He leads the way, walking quickly through the boisterous crowd. His eagerness has my heart beating faster, momentarily overwhelming the sensations of the celebration around us.

I'm mourning the decision to leave the festivities the second we turn onto the quieter Rua Lopes Quintas. Shadows play in my periphery as we head toward my apartment. Relief and unease curl inside me with Kolt's possessive embrace around my midsection.

"Thanks for walking me home," I hedge, already anticipating his disappointment, because I don't think I can go through with it. Not tonight.

We're at my door, and he turns me, squaring our bodies. He weaves his fingers into my hair, caresses over the dampness at the roots, and guides my mouth to his. I accept.

Because if we're not lovers, we're undeniably more than friends. And even though I refuse to give him everything he wants, I still crave contact. His taste is a mirror of sugar and citrus on my tongue. He slides his other hand to the back of my thigh and inches up, pressing his groin to the center of my physical desire. But his desperation barrels over his sensuality.

I close my eyes and reach for what I want... A memory. Silvery-blue eyes flash in my mind. Full lips mark my skin, and then the memory takes me away. In my mind, I'm pinned under hard thrusts that threaten to shatter my body and my heart. Reckless lust and love I want so hard to believe was pure.

A rush of desire hits me. I gasp and answer Kolt's persistent groping with an infinitesimal shift in my hips. With a hungry growl, he pushes me back against the rough stucco of my building. My eyes open to his perfectly chiseled features. I turn my head, disconnecting our mouths. Undeterred, he latches on to my neck instead.

"Kolt...not tonight."

He hitches the tight fabric of my dress up like he means to take me here in the street but stops short of baring me indecently. "Why do you do this to me?" His voice is low, gritty with need.

I wince because I really don't want to do this to him. "If I gave you everything, you wouldn't want it."

He pulls back to stare at me for a quiet moment. "That's a goddamn lie, and you know it. I want you all the time."

He can't want the person he's never truly seen. I trace

my fingers across his lips, wishing I could tell him the truth. That I'm incomplete. Still utterly broken. And he doesn't have what it takes to put me back together. Somehow I know if I told him all that, he'd try to talk me out of it. Either way, the answer isn't the one he wants.

"I drank too much. It doesn't feel right." I offer the half lie that gives him no choice but to leave me alone.

He may be cocky and entitled, but Kolt is still a gentleman. His shoulders soften, and his touch falls away. "At least let me walk you up."

I shake my head. "I'll be fine. I promise."

"Are you sure?"

He's only being half genuine, giving me one last chance to give in. I consider it one more time. I lean in, close the small space between us, and kiss him softly on the mouth.

"Good night, Kolt," I whisper against his lips.

He reacts, taking the kiss deeper, molding his hands over my ass and yanking me against him. I pressure him back gently because we're riding a dangerous edge when it comes to self-control. I still have plenty, but I'm not sure he does.

Finally he lets our bodies separate. His breath comes in uneven pants as he looks me over like every inch of my bare skin burns him.

"Good night, Isabel. I'll see you tomorrow."

Tension lines every plane of his face as he turns and takes brisk strides down the street. He disappears into the shadows I have learned never to trust. I reach for my key, quickly turn it in the lock, and bolt the door behind me.

TRISTAN

Sweat beads down my back. My heart beats slowly, like the pendulum on an old clock. Adrenaline rushes don't come easily for me. As I circle to the rear of the building, memorized details project onto the bright-white screen of my mind.

Isabel Foster. American. English teacher. Aged twenty-five.

Marked for death, she'll be extinguished within the hour. I register the faintest measure of relief that her lover—or the man who desperately wanted to be—is now out of the picture. Collateral damage isn't uncommon, but I prefer to avoid it if I can. God knows I have enough blood on my hands.

I scale the metal stairs in the darkness, mentally mapping my journey from a brief assessment of her living arrangements days ago. The week of Carnaval is already loud and dangerous. Her death will be one of dozens of others reported by the morning.

I peer into her apartment through the glass doors that open from her second-floor balcony. Nearly every light is on. I withdraw my gun from the holster hidden under my shirt. With practiced deftness, I spin the silencer onto the end until it's secure.

Opening the door from her balcony, I pause when a low sound comes from the bedroom. After a beat, I slip inside, leaving the door open a crack for my inevitable departure. I glance around the living room that leads into a small kitchen.

My brain captures snapshots that my photographic memory will store forever, whether I want it to or not. A thriving bromeliad on the window sill. A framed photo of her with her parents. An old purple crocheted blanket strewn over the back of the couch. None of it matters. Tonight will be the last night she draws air.

With that final thought, I move toward her nearly closed bedroom door. The gap reveals my target, but instead of taking action, I halt my advance. Where I didn't care about the sounds of my approach seconds before, now I still my breathing and freeze my motions to become totally silent.

She's on the bed. Her chestnut hair fans out on her lavender pillow, and the sheets are tangled around her ankles. With one hand, she's massaging her breast through the sheer black fabric that clings tightly to it. The other hand is hidden under her panties. Her position reveals details I couldn't have appreciated when I watched her from afar— graceful, toned legs, a line of unreadable text inked along her rib cage, and a smooth, firm stomach decorated with a tiny silver ring pierced through her navel. The pinched look on her face is one I haven't seen before. Not even with her boyfriend. A fascinating mix of anguish and rapture.

With her eyes closed and her position on the bed, she can't know I'm here watching her pleasure herself. The pendulum of my heart swings a little faster at my predicament.

Her beauty doesn't give me pause. A nagging instinct that I know her from somewhere else doesn't give me pause either, though perhaps it should. My weapon hangs heavily at my side now as I entertain both a slow burn of arousal and a rare moment of empathy that I'm about to end her life in the midst of her ecstasy.

I trace my fingertip over the cool metal trigger and attempt to rationalize my hesitation. Then I swiftly resolve to correct it. But not before Isabel's body arches. She wraps her fingers around the edge of the mattress, taking a handful of sheet with her. Her movements quicken, and she sucks in a breath. I'm growing hard, cursing myself with every passing second for my inaction.

Fuck this.

I grit my teeth and lift the gun, lining the barrel up precisely to ensure a quick, painless end.

Her body undulates unevenly as the orgasm rolls through her. She trembles and moans, and my groin betrays the pleasure it's giving me too.

Her lips part with a loud groan and then…

"Tristan…"

My name leaves her lips and fills the room like a gunshot.

I freeze, and the pendulum stops.

JAY: Please report on the status of Isabel Foster.

I chew on a thin red stir straw, rest back into the office chair that sits behind my desk, and stare at the text cursor on my screen. I'm still in disbelief. I've never hesitated like that. I sure as hell have never had a change of heart. I simply have no heart to change.

This was curiosity, pure and simple.

I mash the straw between my molars and quickly type a reply.

RED: In progress. Need
a little more time.

Jay's response comes quickly. I sense her displeasure before the words appear on the computer screen. We've spoken in person only once in three years, and the details are still foggy. She provided only the information that she felt I needed to go into my new life. There was a time when this unnerved me, but now I take solace in it. The less I know, the better. Everyone, including me, is likely safer that way. Except for my marks, of course.

JAY: The client is eager.
Is there a complication?

I hover my fingertips over the keys, weighing my reply. Complications are rare and historically have never required her intervention. Still, I remain irrationally protective of my error, and I want to ensure enough time to fully investigate the source of it.

RED: She has a boyfriend. Waiting to
get her alone so I can keep it clean.

JAY: When will it be done?

RED: Within the week.

I hesitate and follow the answer she doesn't want to hear, trying to allude to inevitable closure on the subject of my living, breathing mark.

RED: Where to next?

JAY: Take care of this
and I'll let you know.

Jay knows I prefer to disappear for a while after a local hit. Rio is vast and crime is rampant, but corruption is being confronted more vigorously, and at least some of the many homicides will receive the thorough investigation they deserve. In addition to being American, Isabel Foster is the daughter of a Pentagon official. Chances are extremely slim, but not impossible, that her death could be linked to my face, my untraceable fingerprints, my unregistered and unmarked car, or my apartment. All in all, incarceration would be easier to avoid if I were nowhere to be found.

After wrestling with my total fuck up all day, I turned my focus to research and compiled a more thorough profile of the girl—an exercise that offered no enlightenment. As far as I can tell, our lives haven't intersected in the past three years. The Tristan on her lips could easily be someone else.

I try to reassure myself that she could be important,

even if I don't understand why yet. Then I remind myself that Isabel Foster is a beautiful woman who shouted my name as she brought herself to orgasm, and there is not a single iota of importance to that odd coincidence. I am being idiotic, male, and uncharacteristically human. Yet I stare at the photograph before me, and all of my instincts—all the ones that have kept me alive through God knows how many situations that certainly should have left me dead—tell me unequivocally that my hesitation has merit.

I blink a few times and type into the protected chat that allows both Jay and me anonymity, never knowing each other's exact whereabouts. We deal in death wishes and wire transfers, with not a shred of trust between us.

RED: A hint?

I try for humor, knowing Jay has none. Still, having something to look forward to would be welcome. Rio is becoming intolerable. Sensory overload. Easy to blend in, impossible to tune out. I've had the strong urge to move on for months. Perhaps now is the time. Now, when I've faltered so irrationally, risking everything.

Yes, I'd move on after this. I'd take Jay's next assignment, scout my next stop, and say goodbye to Brazil for a while.

JAY: How is your Russian?

I smirk. Jay's reply is both humor and insult. She knows my language skills are shit and I hate the cold. I've never said no, though.

RED: Flawless as always.
I'll be in touch.

I close out the chat and pace the largely empty living room. Nearly every square foot of my apartment is dedicated to my work. The space contains an old teacher's desk covered with connected monitors. A leather chair sits in the corner. The walls are cluttered with notes, all currently dedicated to the inauspicious woman who is hijacking my thoughts at the moment.

I have no need for couches or formal dining areas. Or friends, family, or lovers. I've never had a guest, and I suspect I never will.

I'm going to find out why Isabel Foster's face feels like it's been tattooed onto my brain. I'm going to eliminate her. And then I'm going to leave this country without a trace.

2

ISABEL

"I'm going to the store. Can I get you anything?"

I overenunciate each word and take in the wide-eyed stares from my classroom of students. They attend the Horizonte Centre to learn English, and I have the unfair advantage of being fluent in their native language as well as my own.

Ramona, a teenager from a nearby secondary school, raises her hand. "Can you get for me a loaf of bread?"

I smile because she's progressed quickly in my class but also because I recognize my drive in her. That drive to excel, paired with an affinity for language, had in some ways saved me. Language had healed me. Ultimately, it had given me a ticket to run away.

"Of course. Anything else?"

I glance around the room for other participants. I sense someone's eyes on me and turn my head. Kolt is standing in the doorway. He looks fresh wearing his expensive blue jeans, a pale-blue collared shirt, and a cocky grin, as if I didn't blatantly shoot him down just hours ago.

"*Bom dia, amigos.*" He flits his gaze around the classroom and then nods to me, his smirk deepening. "*Senhorita Foster.*"

I want to be mad, but he makes it difficult. I can only muster mild annoyance. "English only in my classroom, Mr. Mirchoff."

"Lunch?"

I want to admonish him for clearly flirting with me in front of my students. They smile and share knowing looks. I think they enjoy this pretend romance that most of the school and its staff believe we have. I think they also enjoy when I play hard to get.

"We have ten more minutes of class. I suggest you get back to work. *Tchau.*"

I flip my hand in his direction and move to the whiteboard to highlight some new vocabulary.

"Now, who brought their recipe homework today?"

Twenty minutes later, I'm sitting across from Kolt at the outdoor café. I'm devouring my sandwich while he picks at a pastry beside an emptied cup of coffee.

"How are you feeling?"

I look up, wide-eyed. "I'm fine, why?"

He follows the curve of the cup with his finger. "Well,

after all those caipirinhas last night, I thought it might be a rough morning for you."

I pretend like I don't hear him. We both know the truth anyway.

"Can I take you out tonight? Dinner maybe?"

I shake my head. "The city is too crazy right now. Maybe next week sometime after things calm down."

That would also buy me time to figure out what to do with him. Because a real relationship isn't in the cards for me right now.

He works his jaw and stares at me intently. I'm worried he can read my thoughts. I've never been great at schooling my features.

"Isabel, what's going on with us? We work together. We're friends, and we messed around a few times. Now I don't know what we are."

I swallow hard and avoid his gaze. "I don't like labels."

"Fuck buddies?"

I glare at him. "Stop."

He shrugs his shoulders. "Sorry. I'm not trying to be an asshole, but I can't stop thinking about what I want this to be." He gestures between us, his expression softening.

"Kolt…" I sigh because it's safer than forming words. I like our easy friendship. I enjoy the low hum of our attraction. But I can't get entangled with him.

"Is there someone else back home?" Concern shadows his eyes.

I shake my head. "He's gone."

His lips tighten. "Who is he?"

"Nobody. An old flame. It was a long time ago, but he's not the problem. I'm the problem."

"You're perfect." Affection and determination wrap around his words, tugging at my heart.

At this moment I hate Kolt for being sweet and charming. I hate myself for not being able to embrace it, because if I could, that means I could be normal. I could fall in love, make love, and carve out a normal future with a man like him. But I'm not healed all the way, and I'm not certain I ever will be.

"I'm so far from perfect, you have no idea."

I distract myself by watching the people on the street. Every walk of life. Every wild and passionate inclination fueled by this week's celebrations. I belong to this city more than I'll ever belong to Kolt. Even though it challenges me and scares the shit out of me sometimes.

On the other side of the street, a man dressed in black is leaning against the building. In black jeans, black T-shirt, and a faded green jacket, he seems to be the only one not in motion. I can't look away. Something about his face commands my attention. The longer I look, the faster my heart beats. So fast and so loud that I can't hear Kolt speaking above it.

I'm riveted. I'm in disbelief.

"Isabel?"

I tear my gaze away to meet Kolt's. "What?" I snap at him, because I can't help how annoyed I suddenly feel by this conversation and his untimely distractions.

He leans in and reaches for my hand. "All I'm asking

for is a chance to talk this through over dinner."

"Fine, dinner." I pull my hand away and look back to the man in the street. Fear seizes my heart. He's gone.

No, no, no.

How could I have lost him? Seconds have gone by. Only seconds. I grab my purse and throw some bills on the table.

Kolt frowns. "Where are you going?"

"I'm sorry. I just have to go." I push up from the table and walk away. I scan up and down the street. My breath hitches when I catch a glimpse of the man's green jacket disappearing behind a group of partiers several feet away.

I don't think. I move as quickly as the crush of the street traffic allows.

"Tristan!" I yell, garnering a few looks from passersby.

He doesn't look back. My heart falls.

It has to be him. It has to be. Otherwise I'm crazy.

My thoughts whirl and stutter. Maybe I have lost my mind. Maybe that's how badly he's broken me. That's how desperately I want him back. I've dreamed him up so many nights, he's going to haunt my goddamn days now too.

The seconds seems to grow longer as that last thought passes through my mind. He's disappeared again. No matter how hard I look or fast I move, he's nowhere to be found.

My gut is telling me he's close. My whole body is telling me I need to find him again. Except I feel like I'm running out of time.

I pass salons and stores and run-down nothingness. I scan faces and peer down alleys. I don't know how far I've gone or how much time has passed, but as hope dwindles, a familiar pain stabs at my heart.

Loss. Regret. Utter loneliness.

I should turn back. I should go back to my life and forget the dream…banish the memory…heal my heart.

TRISTAN

I'm rioting inside. She knows me. She screamed my name down the street, for fuck's sake.

Determined to prove my gut was all wrong about Isabel Foster, I decided to see her up close. Resolve once and for all that there was nothing special about her so I could kill her and move on with my plan to get out of Rio and on to my next assignment. I had no idea I'd be tempting fate.

I've been traveling the globe for three years. Working, blending in, and then getting out of sight. No one's ever given me a second glance. No one's ever known my name. I'm a ghost, and with one look, this woman has pulled me from a life of anonymity. I don't know how to wrap my head around this new reality. It's both terrifying and too tempting to deny.

If she knows me…

God, the possibilities are endless. My life is a book ripped in half. The first few hundred pages forever lost. But what if they aren't?

I can see her clearly from inside the restaurant I ducked into moments ago. She's stopped in the middle of the busy street, only a few feet away, wringing her hands and looking everywhere. *Looking for me.*

She turns her back to me. Her shoulders hunch. I can almost feel her ready to give up. I should let her. I should finish this, but there's no way I can now. In the space of a few seconds, she's graduated from a mark to the most fascinating person I've ever known.

I step out of the shadows of the restaurant and onto the sidewalk. She spins as if she senses me there. Our gazes lock. She says my name again, and another explosion of panic detonates. I can hardly fucking breathe.

I pivot quickly, continue up the street, and turn into a narrow alley. Darkness closes in on me the farther I walk. The alley is empty, quieter than the busy street. I can hear her footsteps behind me. Then her voice.

"Tristan!"

I turn back, and she halts a couple feet away. I've been watching her from afar for days. Being this close to someone I'm supposed to take out typically means they're about to say their last words. This is different. So very different.

"Oh my God. I never thought I'd see you again." Her eyes are glassy, and her voice trembles. "It's me… Isabel."

She reaches for me, and I'm ready to jump out of my skin. I cover her mouth with my hand and press her to the alley wall. She puffs rapidly into my hand, confusion washing her beautiful features. Her stormy hazel eyes are red-rimmed, but she doesn't struggle against me.

"Who knows about me?"

I drop my hand so she can speak. Her rose-colored lips

part, but she remains silent. Is she in shock? Why do I want to kiss her? Why does seeing her cry twist something inside me?

Not knowing fills me with renewed frustration. The muscles in my jaw tense, and I grit out the next words. "Tell me. Who knows I'm here?"

She shakes her head quickly. "No one."

I exhale in relief. "No one can know."

As I say it, I realize I can't trust her to stay quiet now that she's seen me.

"Are you in trouble, Tristan? Is everything okay?"

A shockwave jolts through me every time she says my name. It's making me edgy. This woman's presence had me unsettled from day one. If I don't find out why, she'll haunt me forever. I need to find out what she knows about me. I need more time. Except every day she's breathing is a day we're both at risk.

I've given her more time than she deserves. She's supposed to be dead. I'm not about to let her get me killed too.

Back on the street, pedestrians stream by unaware and unconcerned with us. I have to make a decision. Kill her now or satisfy curiosity about my past that's never burned this fiercely.

3

ISABEL

Tristan's voice is like cold velvet—rich with texture, void of feeling. I'm a trembling mess, but his eyes are calm.

He's bigger than I remember. His clothes hint at the solid muscular frame beneath. He's changed, but I'd know him anywhere. Those piercing eyes, opalescent blue orbs that I could stare into for the rest of my life. His hair is the same dark brown, short and unstyled. Stubble lines his jaw, making the ridges of his full lips stand out. Worry lines crease his forehead and the edges of his eyes.

We've grown. We're not the same.

A thousand thoughts blur together as I convince myself he's not a dream. No longer just a memory.

He's Tristan Stone. The love of my life.

He takes a step back, and the separation borders on painful.

Instinct drives me next. My fingers become ten tiny magnets. I reach for him, drawn to his flesh, determined to prove he's not an apparition. Before I can make contact, he takes my wrists in a firm grasp, holding them immobile in the horrible empty space between us. Those few inches are made up of years of missing him. Of not knowing if he was alive or dead.

"You're looking at me like you hardly know me." I choke on the last word because every emotion is tearing its way up my throat.

His expression never changes. He's unreadable. "I know who you are, Isabel."

I let go of the fight in my muscles, feeling foolish and broken all over again. He doesn't love me anymore. I'm so far in the past, how could he have possibly hung on to those feelings like I have?

"We should go," he says, releasing his hold on me.

I drop my hands to my sides, confused and reeling from everything that's happening between us. True enough, this alley isn't the safest place for a reunion.

"Where do you want to go?"

"Your place. I'm parked nearby. I'll drive us."

I swallow my doubts and follow him down the alley to the congested street. He tugs me behind him until we get to his car. He opens the passenger door and shuts it after me without ceremony.

Seconds later, Tristan is whipping through the streets. I can't imagine the reason for his urgency.

"How long have you been in Rio?"

"A while." He glances into the rearview mirror, seeming distracted.

I nod and try to ignore the sting of his tone. I remember a gentler Tristan. Always tuned in to my feelings and needs. The man I met in the street is frighteningly intense and completely unreadable.

He stops at the end of my street, puts the car in park, and turns to me.

"How do you know where I live?" My heart starts racing again at this new revelation.

"There's no time to talk. Not here. I need you to pack a bag for a few days away," he says.

"A few days? I can't just leave with you. I have a job." I can no longer hide the panic in my voice.

He stares at me silently for a moment and then speaks slowly and calmly. "I know it doesn't make sense. I have a friend outside the city. We'll stay with him, and I can explain everything there."

I blink slowly, trying to process his proposal. "Then we'll come back?"

He nods wordlessly. I don't completely believe him, but I'm not willing to let him disappear again so soon.

"I need to call work."

He opens his palm. "Give me your phone."

I reach into my purse and hand it to him, expecting him to make a call with it. Instead he puts it into his coat pocket.

"You have five minutes. You can make your calls on the road."

My throat tightens, and my eyes burn with fresh tears. "Tristan…you're scaring me."

"Five minutes." His voice is clipped. "Go now."

I reach for the car door, feeling numb but propelled forward by Tristan's inexplicable urgency. He pulls out his phone, and I step out just as he begins to speak into it.

"Mateus. I need a favor."

I hurry to my apartment. My hands are shaking as I turn the key in the lock. I rush up the stairs and pull a backpack out of my closet. I glance at the clock, and the urge to cry is almost too strong to resist.

What the fuck am I doing? Tristan just crash-landed back into my world. After the most agonizing goodbye of my life when he joined the army all those years ago. After one last heartbreaking letter saying we were over. After years of nothing but silence and heartache.

He's a stranger, yet he never could be. Not after everything we went through together. And now we're thousands of miles from a home we once knew, and I'm agreeing to leave with him. It's only a few days, but this is insane.

I keep moving through my doubt as I stuff clothes into the bag. A few toiletries. I kneel to the floor and open the lockbox under my bed. I empty it of my passport and some cash and put both into the backpack.

I scan the bedroom and living room briefly. Why does dropping everything and running off seem justifiable when the love of my life is idling at the end of the street, waiting to drive us into a future unknown?

TRISTAN

All my loose plans for leaving Rio just firmed up. I can't let Isabel out of my sight, so the only option is to bring her into my world. Doesn't matter what she ends up seeing anyway. Her days are numbered. Hell, at this rate, mine are too.

We drive away from her neighborhood toward the condo-lined strip of Ipanema Beach. We pull into the parking lot of my building and take the elevator to the penthouse condo in silence.

She takes one step inside and freezes. "You live here?"

"I mostly work." Not a lot of living happens inside these walls. I shut the door behind us and shift both deadbolts to the side. As if in a daze, she wanders toward the sliding doors that lead to the oceanfront balcony. I register faint regret that it's probably the last time I'll have this view. The waves crash silently on the beach below as I eye her warily. So far she's gone along with everything, but I have a feeling the window of her compliance is closing.

I go to my desk and start moving through my mental checklist. I remotely back up my files and wipe the machines. I pull papers and photos pinned to the wall and stuff them into a folder.

In the bedroom, I find the lever inside the chest of drawers that rests along an accent wall. The large mirror above it angles up, and I push it open the rest of the way, revealing a hidden compartment that stores possessions I wouldn't want anyone knowing about. I pull an array of weapons off the pegs that display them and throw them into a bag. Beside several bricks of cash in various currencies, my passports are bound with a thick rubber band to a worn red leather notebook. I collect what I need, grab clothes, and make my way back to Isabel.

Except she's no longer there. That, and the room *feels* empty without her in it somehow. The folder on my desk is open, revealing pictures of her, her boyfriend, her work schedule, and a few other documents I collected.

The door is open. *Fuck.*

I grab the folder and my bags and say goodbye to the apartment and everything in it. In the hallway, numbers illuminate above the elevator bank. She's on her way down. I hurry to the stairs. I won't beat her, but she's got nowhere to go.

Heat and ocean air hit my lungs the second I emerge from the building. I'm parked close, and Isabel's already at the car, struggling with the door. I come from behind.

"What the hell are you doing?" I force myself to keep an even tone.

She whips around. Her eyes are wide, and her pupils are dilated. "Let me have my things."

I open the trunk and deposit my bag. "Get in the car."

"I'm not going with you."

She's practically screaming, so I take her firmly by the arm and lead her to the passenger side. She struggles, but I won't let her go. A few more feet and we'll be on our way without making a scene.

"Why do you have all those things about me? How could you be here, this close to me all this time? I need answers, Tristan!"

I open the door, but she fights me.

I lean her against the car and take a handful of her hair, tilting her face up to mine. Before she can say anything more, I'm kissing her. Her hands go to my shoulders, but she's no match for my strength. I kiss her until I feel her fight go.

A small sound escapes her, disappearing in the melding of our lips. My eyes barely close, because I don't trust her, or anyone. As her tongue seeks mine, her flavor floods my senses. Sweet and fresh. Soft surrender. She holds nothing back, so neither do I. I kiss her deeper to take in more of her essence. As I do, my eyes close.

Then she's on the bright-white screen of my mind. The visual is overexposed, like a memory. She's under me. Her body moves with mine. We're fucking. I can feel her everywhere. She's overwhelming all my senses. The fantasy takes hold and arousal prickles my skin—everywhere we touch and everywhere we don't.

Except it all feels too real. Feels too good to be a fantasy. In seconds, my body begins to respond to the closeness of hers. Which is just fucking great.

I can already see this will be yet another distraction I can't afford. I was hired to kill this woman. Now I'm about to kidnap her and keep her until she can tell me things I'm not yet sure I want to know. And all I can think about is getting inside her.

There's no time for this.

I break the kiss and try to mentally erase the disturbing erotic image. But Isabel replaces it in the flesh, breathless, her eyes hazy. She looks how I feel. Overwhelmed. Confused. Ready to fuck.

The pulse at her neck beats rapidly. She might be turned on, but she's scared too. And even if she thinks she knows me, she's too smart to give me her trust. I only need a little of it to get us out of here.

I brush her hair back off her face. I'm not accustomed to charming my way to a desired end, but I manage a small reassuring smile. "I need you to trust me. Okay?"

She softens, but I keep my hold on her.

"I want to," she utters.

It has to be enough. I don't ask, and I don't tell her again. I simply guide her into the car, shut the door, and move back to the driver's seat.

As I start the ignition, I'm anything but relieved.

Two hours go by, and already the drive is too long. Isabel's presence dominates the small space of the car and every crevice of my mind. She chews her lower lip and wrings her fingers as the city turns into jungle and the road narrows. Her fear and uncertainty don't affect me. The longing in her eyes does. Her confusion seems laced with an affection I can't comprehend.

She has questions, and so do I. I have no idea how I'll answer hers. I wasn't prepared for this. I grip the wheel and cycle through my options.

Killing her would have been so much easier. I've built this new life on the surety of the kill. The simplicity of it.

Nothing is simple now.

I keep my eyes straight ahead. "We know each other."

A statement. A question.

I could spend days coaxing the truth out of her, pretending to know about whatever connection we share. But if I have to kill her anyway—and despite my strong urge to fuck her, I *will* have to kill her—the truth can do no harm. I realize this in a moment of sudden clarity.

I brave a look in her direction. She stares back in confused silence.

"Of course we do."

I break the stare and focus on the road. "How?"

I refuse to meet her gaze again. The late-afternoon sun is setting ahead of us, turning the sky orange and mauve above the trees as we pass through town after town.

"You know…"

I shake my head slightly. "I have gaps"—I swallow hard, pushing down the unwelcome feeling that comes with the truth—"pretty big gaps in my memory. I recognize you. I just have no idea why."

I can feel her gaze hot on me. The air between us is thick with emotions neither of us can fully understand. I turn, and the tears in her eyes confirm the pain I've inflicted with this admission.

"We were in love," she utters, almost too quietly to be heard.

I curse inwardly. Another complication I don't need.

"When?"

"It's been six years since you left."

"Since I left?"

"You joined the military right out of high school. I went to college, but you never came home."

I nod slowly. She's an old girlfriend. From high school, for fuck's sake. Nothing. She's nothing. Lovesick and naïve, thanks to a narrow, privileged existence. If she were important, surely she'd have been *somewhere* in my memories. Somewhere in the dreams or nightmares, the smallest flashes of remembrance, the blurred darkness that is my past.

My stomach clenches. My grip tightens around the wheel. The urge to dig through those clues and learn more is dangerous. For years, I've existed for no other reason than to breathe, point, and shoot. Even if Jay hasn't all but promised it, inherently, I've always known that reaching beyond that basic state of being is inevitably painful and likely to end in death. Not others' for once, but mine. Yet here I am, seeking out my past. Drawn to the irresistible beacon of Isabel Foster and the things she knows about me.

"If you don't remember me…how did you know where to find me?"

I make a turn onto a dirt road and ease off the gas. Outside of Jay and the people whose light left their eyes at my hand, very few people know exactly what I do. Mateus knows enough to be an ally. I trust him because I did him a favor once, and now he owes me about a thousand in return.

Ahead, a pristine white stucco house is set back on a large lot protected by several feet of well-kept gardens and a wrought-iron gate. I slow at the entrance and dial Mateus's number.

He answers after the first ring. "Tristan?"

"I'm here."

The call ends and the gates, armed by guards on either side, slowly open. I pull through and drive up the winding path to the house. Every inch closer brings an unexpected calm over my rattled nerves. A momentary reprieve is what I need, and I'll find it here.

4

ISABEL

I've never been this far outside the city. Every instinct is shouting at me. It's the same voice that keeps me on high alert when I'm in uncharted territory or edging outside my comfort zone. Tristan leaves the vehicle and pops the trunk, while I hold on to the door handle with a white-knuckled grip. What if this was all a terrible mistake?

I want to trust him. I told him so, but that was two seconds after he kissed me like the Tristan I remember. The second our lips touched, an avalanche of memories rushed in. Stolen moments, heated touches, and forbidden nights. Everything precious that clung to the hurt he'd caused me, making him impossible to forget.

In my periphery, a man descends the white stone steps that lead to the grand entrance of the home. He smiles warmly, and I hear his muffled greeting to Tristan from inside the car. I take a deep breath, gather my resolve, and step out.

"It's good to see you, *meu amigo*." The man's gaze shifts swiftly to me. "And who is this?" His accent is thick and brusque.

"I'm Isabel." I smile weakly and take his outstretched hand to shake it.

In one fluid motion, he brings it to his lips and brushes a kiss against my skin. The warmth in his dark eyes chases away the discomfort the gesture should give me. The man has charm, and even though my entire life changed a few hours ago, somehow I'm grateful we're here and not someplace even more frightening.

"I'm Mateus da Silva. *Muito prazer em conhecê-la.* Welcome to my home."

"*Obrigada*," I mutter.

Tristan's eyes darken as he hauls our bags over his shoulder. "Shall we?"

"Of course." Mateus hesitates a moment before easing away, nodding toward Tristan, and leading us toward the house.

We step inside onto a well-worn Persian rug that stretches into an expansive living area. The walls are covered with dozens of paintings of varying sizes. Each is trimmed with gold leaf and light dust. Antique furniture hugs the walls and completes several small entertaining areas. The tables are decorated with ornate lamps and bronze statues.

The guards at the gate and the heavily barred windows

tell me whatever he keeps in this house is worth protecting. I'm telling myself it has to do with the wall-to-wall antiques and nothing to do with the danger that Tristan insists we're running from.

"Are you hungry from your travels? I can have a meal prepared."

"We'll eat in the room," Tristan answers quickly. "Where are we staying?"

Mateus motions us to follow him down a hall. He seems unaffected by Tristan's grim mood. A sinking feeling washes over me. If this is normal behavior for Tristan, who has he become? Is there anything left of the man I fell in love with so many years ago? I can't think that way...

We pause outside one of the doors, which Mateus pushes open. "The honeymoon suite," he says with a smirk.

Tristan frowns but doesn't reply. He only guides me into the room that matches the rest of the house—rich textures and deep colors. The bed is draped in a red satin bedspread, its ornate metal headboard pressed to the wall like a piece of art in itself.

"I will have Karina bring you dinner. I'll be in the den if you need me, Tristan."

"Thank you," Tristan says after dropping our bags to the floor. He meets Mateus's gaze briefly, and I swear something passes between them. An understanding, a wordless exchange.

"Good night, Isabel." Mateus bows his head before retreating, leaving us alone again.

I walk to the window. Through the bars, all I can see are

trees and the winding drive up to the house. I wrap my arms around myself and turn to face Tristan.

"Are you going to give me my phone now?"

My first two requests were refused, which only ramped up my panic on the ride here.

"Not yet."

I tense with renewed anxiety. Then I remind myself that I know Tristan. Maybe he doesn't know me, but once upon a time, he was a man I could trust. A good man.

"I left with you without telling anyone. I have a job and a life and friends who—"

"I'm sure your boyfriend can live without you for a few days." He stands in the middle of the room with his arms crossed. The muscles in his jaw tighten, and the air becomes thick with tension I don't understand.

Then I remember the photos of Kolt and me together in his file. "Are you talking about Kolt?"

He shrugs slightly. "The American who can't keep his hands off you."

My cheeks heat like I've been caught doing something wrong. "Kolt isn't my boyfriend."

He lifts an eyebrow but otherwise maintains an inexpressive countenance. In an instant, I want him to be jealous, because it means something still exists between us. He was so possessive once. So convinced that we were meant to be together, two halves of a whole that no amount of time or distance could keep apart.

I drop my hands to my sides. "Would you care if he were?"

"No," he says flatly.

His blunt answer lashes back at me, reward for an indulgent moment of yearning for his affection again after such an absence. "What do you want from me, Tristan?"

He stares at me a moment before turning toward the crushed-velvet couch that lines one wall of the room. He sits down and drops his head into his hands. "I'm still trying to figure that out."

For the first time since he kissed me, I sense his vulnerability. I fight the urge to go to him and wrap my arms around him. My fingers itch to touch him. But what good can my touch do when he doesn't know me? I still can't fathom that our entire history has been erased. A part of me refuses to believe it's true.

I swallow over the painful tightness in my throat. "What really happened to you?"

"I don't know very much," he says. "When I woke up… Everything was kind of a blur. Jay—" A deep groove cuts between his dark brows. "I had been on a tour overseas, on a special ops team. A mission went wrong…really wrong. I guess it was bad enough that my life in the military was over and my freedom would be in jeopardy if I didn't disappear. Someone on the inside pulled strings to give me a second chance. A chance to start over as someone else."

"When did this happen?"

"Three years ago. Everything before that…it's just flashes. So small that I can't tell if it's real or just my imagination. Kind of like a dream you can't fully remember."

The last letter from Tristan had come to me six months

after his enlistment. Long before this incident occurred. When he said goodbye and ended things between us, he had his memory. Six agonizing years compound onto my heart. The emotional pain turns physical as my chest constricts and pinpricks cut into my palms.

He looks up at me, his eyes clear and wide. For the first time, I'm convinced of the emptiness of his memories. I push my pain away and reach for compassion. If he brought us here to fill in the gaps, I'm probably the only one who can help.

"Why did you bring me here?"

His lips thin and his features tighten. "It's not safe for you in Rio. Not anymore."

I jump at a knock at the door. Tristan rises as a beautiful young woman arrives with a tray full of dishes in her arms. He relieves her of it, and she closes the door. He sets the tray on the table by the bed and gestures toward it.

"Eat." He turns away and shoves his hands into his pockets.

"Aren't you hungry?"

"No."

I huff, cross my arms, and ignore the pang in my stomach. I powered through my lunch, but the stress of the afternoon and the hours passed have me starving. Still, bigger issues loom. I'm not ready to accept his silence and avoidance.

"You need to talk to me, Tristan. You can't leave me in the dark."

He spins back, his eyes narrowed. "In the dark? My past

is pitch black, Isabel."

I hesitate, momentarily thrown by his anger. "I'm sorry, but—"

"You're sorry? You have no idea who or what you're dealing with." His tone is low and, if I didn't know better, threatening. "And I don't need your goddamn pity. Eat your dinner."

My temper flares at his words. In an instant, I forget that Tristan is essentially a stranger off the street. I push to my feet and get so close our faces are mere inches apart.

"You either talk to me or I'm going home. I don't care how dangerous you say it is."

I expect anger, but his expression flattens into a hard calm. Somehow that's even scarier.

"You're not leaving here, Isabel."

There's something final about his tone, nearly knocking the wind out of me.

I maneuver past him and go for my bag. Before I can get to it, he's between me and the door.

"I don't think you heard me. You're *not* leaving."

I place my hands on his chest to push him away, but the second I attempt it, I'm stumbling backward. He bands his arms around my torso, dragging us toward the bed. My hands are free, so I pound against his shoulders and struggle against his massive strength.

"Let me go! Let me go, or I'll scream!"

I'm already yelling, but he doesn't seem to care. My heart is racing, and hateful tears burn behind my eyes. Inside, I'm at war with my innate trust in him and the fear he inspires.

Any possibility of escape is squashed when I realize he's got me entirely immobile—hands around my wrists and his hard, heavy body pinning me flat to the bed, my legs kicking feebly off the edge. He repositions my wrists into one of his hands, reaches behind his back, and retrieves a sliver of plastic.

I scream and pray that Mateus's earlier affection might save me now.

But he never shows, and Tristan has deftly cinched each wrist to the metal bedposts. The cable tie is thin enough to sting me when I test it but thick enough that I don't have a chance of breaking it without really hurting myself.

As quickly as he secured me, he lifts off me twice as fast. He paces once around the room.

"Why are you doing this?" My voice is weak and watery. I can't fight him now. I can only appeal to his humanity.

He stops and pivots in my direction. His eyes are ice. No shred of the man I knew. A second later, he's out the door and I'm alone. I cry and then I scream. I scream until my throat burns. Until the sky fades into a black night and sleep overwhelms me.

TRISTAN

"Who is the girl?"

Mateus shuffles barefoot toward the sideboard that holds a few bottles of his favorite liquors and a set of cut glasses. His linen clothing hangs loosely on his short and stocky frame. His calm expression and easy movements are perfectly relaxed. He's at home, appearing so comfortable that I have no choice but to feel at home myself, as much as I ever could.

Part of Mateus's gift is his ability to put people at ease. That's also what makes him lethal. No one ever sees him coming.

"No one of importance, as far as I can tell," I say.

An old girlfriend. I chastise myself for this new fact as a smirk curves Mateus's cheek.

"You don't expect me to believe that, do you?"

He brings me a tumbler of clear liquid muddled with limes. One sniff, and I identify the local brand of cachaça. The essence of sugarcane fills my mouth, but the lime clears it away, inviting me to another taste. I swallow, welcome the sensation, and exhale a sigh.

I close my eyes and think about her taste. The way it consumed me when I had it on my tongue. Then doubt and rational thought wash it away.

When I open my eyes, Mateus is sitting on the adjacent couch watching me. Tan leather cracked with wear and use slides under his palm as he rests it on the arm.

"She is very beautiful," he says.

I nod. Isabel's beauty is indisputable. I just wish it was the only thing drawing me to her.

"She looks at you like you are precious to her. I had no idea such a creature could exist in your world."

I take another swallow and weigh my next words. Everything about this situation is uncomfortable for me. My past is foreign soil, a battleground I've never seen before. I'm unarmed and completely unready for it.

"I knew her once," I finally admit.

"And now you are protecting her?"

"The opposite, actually."

I don't need to say any more. Mateus can put the pieces together. He frowns, and his lips form a wrinkled line.

"I see. So why have you brought her here?"

"I need time. She knows things…" I pinch the bridge of my nose, still uncertain how long it'll take for me to explore this newfound curiosity about my past. "Someone will notice she's gone soon enough. Probably her boyfriend or her coworkers. Then her family back in the States will know something's gone wrong. I don't have much time. You don't have to worry. We won't be here long."

He sweeps his hand in a gesture between us. "You can stay as long as you need to."

"I won't make this your mess. Not in your home."

He lifts an eyebrow and cocks his head. "If you must, you know I will oblige. Even if it costs me this refuge. My debt has not been paid."

"I'm in no rush for you to pay it." Calling Mateus's debt over this would be foolish. I may have left Rio in a rush, but I still have time and space to maneuver.

Mateus sighs heavily. "Perhaps one day, if the devil doesn't take us too soon, you'll tell me your story."

I muster a laugh. "Perhaps if I knew it, I'd tell you."

Mateus's eyes soften with understanding. We've hardly bared our souls to one another, but he knows my past is beyond reach. Oddly I think he counts my anonymity as an asset to our friendship.

"If your past is dark, how do you know who she is?"

I pause and relive that moment of recognition as she sat in the café this afternoon. Life had been different seconds before.

"She recognizes me. She knows me." I frown hard. "We were lovers. She hasn't forgotten, and I have no way of remembering."

"*Meu Deus*, Tristan! How can you let her go?" Mateus's cool calm breaks as he leans forward, resting his forearms on his thighs.

I shrug. "It's her or me."

He cusses under his breath and rises to his feet. He crosses the long room, opens a drawer at his desk, and returns.

"Here," he says, pushing a blackened silver frame into my hands.

I open it like a book, and it parts stiffly. Inside, two ornately trimmed ovals reveal faded photographs. On each side, a woman and a man are dressed in clothing from a couple generations past.

I lift my gaze to him. "Your parents?"

He nods. "My sister raised me. My father opposed the regime, so they burned down our home. My parents were tied down, brutalized while my sister and I sneaked away. We couldn't save them. Days later, we found this in the rubble. A miracle." He's silent a moment, his gaze on the frame. "Their enemies wanted them to disappear. No body, no voice, no grave beyond the ashes of our home. But this…" He leans in and drops his thick fingertip onto the center of his mother's photograph. "This is a memory they could not destroy."

When he pulls back, I close the frame gently and hand it back to him. "You're lucky to have found it."

He whips it from my grasp. "And you, *idiota*, are lucky to have her. She is your memory. She is your living and breathing miracle." He shakes the frame at me once more before returning it back to his desk, slamming the drawer firmly shut.

He returns and drops on the couch. I marvel at Mateus's break in composure. I've only seen him beyond reason one other time. Those were memories neither of us wished to relive. But this is different. He's emotional over memories he holds. I have nothing like that.

"She's going to get me killed," I finally say. Suddenly, despite everything I've told myself, I know this to be true. Isabel is difficult and impulsive. No reasonable person would leave her life behind on a whim to come with me—a stranger. She's unpredictable and far too attached to the person I once was. And already I can feel her reaching for more.

Mateus rests his empty glass on the table beside him and spins it rhythmically.

"People are always wishing away their bad memories. *Meu Deus, I wish I could forget. Make it go away.* Ah!" He flicks his hand. "They only wish away the pain it brings them. Me? I would rather die than live as you have, Tristan. Nothing but death to drive you forward. If hers will keep you on this path, you have nothing to live for."

I hold my teeth together, bearing down against the impact of his words. "And what do you live for? Vengeance? How is that life better?"

Mateus's expression relaxes a fraction. "Tristan… You are vengeance for hire, for those who don't have the heart or the *colhões* to pull the trigger themselves."

I down the rest of my drink and rise to my feet. I pace around the room, chasing the flurry of thoughts that accuse and contradict and provide no true answers. Mateus is perhaps my only friend, and he could be right. If Isabel dies, by my hand or any other, her memories of my life die with her.

I shove my hands through my hair with a pained sound. Why do I fucking care? Living with darkness might not be a life worth living, but it was vastly simpler. Nothing is simple now.

"Tristan."

I turn as Mateus speaks. His eyes are soft with understanding, but everything else—his posture, the tension that lines his shoulders—speaks of his newfound determination to guide me through this.

"Go to her. She has the answers."

5

TRISTAN

A small click and the pelt of rain against the windows are the only sounds as I enter the room. Isabel is asleep. Her body lies diagonally on the bare bed. The satin bedspread and sheets have been kicked to the floor. Suspended by the restraints, her arms are stretched above her, obscuring her face.

I switch on the lamp beside the couch. The tray of dishes remains untouched, and I'm momentarily grateful Karina didn't return for them while I was gone. Isabel would have begged to be freed, unknowing that Karina is also Mateus's lover and would never betray him.

I circle the bed without a sound, gaining a better view of Isabel's face. Dried tears streak her cheeks. Her lips and eyes are puffy. I don't enjoy the misery that's only just begun for her. She's trapped here, but so am I.

Every hour that passes with her in my world awakens compassion I didn't know I possessed. I resent her for it, even if I can't deny it.

I retrieve a knife from my pocket and cut through the plastic bonds. Her eyes open wide. She scrambles away from me the second she's free enough to move. She glances around the room and then down at her wrists, which are red and will likely bruise by morning. She rubs them but says nothing.

"I'm sorry," I finally say.

She laughs roughly. "You're sorry?"

"If you understood the danger we're in, you'd know leaving here without me is impossible."

She swallows but doesn't meet my eyes. "If you explained why we're in danger, maybe I wouldn't have wanted to leave."

I reach for her, but she flinches back. She slides her stormy gaze to mine. Slowly, I take her hand, tracing the grooves at her wrist with my thumb.

I slide my hand into hers. I don't know why I do it. But the contact, palm to palm, sends a shockwave over my nerves. It's not the vague familiarity I've experienced before with her. It's something more...something primal...deeper.

Her gaze settles there. Her lips part, as if she feels it too.

"You have something valuable of mine," I say. "I have to protect you, even if that means protecting you from yourself sometimes. You'll have to forgive me because I'm not in the business of protecting anyone. You'll just have to learn to trust me."

She doesn't show acceptance in any way. She only stares at me. The mix of concern and devotion passing over her features is troubling, making me feel like a stranger in my own skin.

Exhaustion tugs at my body. Knowing she could run, or worse, will make it difficult to drift off, but the thought of lying down beside her promises something soothing.

"Come on. Let's get some sleep."

I get up and replace the blankets on the bed. I kick off my shoes and untuck my gun, placing it on the bedside table nearest to me. I hear Isabel's sharp intake of breath before I catch the fear in her eyes.

"For protection," I say, reassuring her. And myself.

I take life day by day, hour by hour. Everything could change tomorrow. But right now, she's safe with me.

I move around the tiny kitchen. She'll be home soon, and I'll have food ready for her before I head to school. She's been working all night.

That's when I hear it. Gunshots. The familiar sound freezes me in place. My heart stops beating. They're too close.

I fly to the door. Her car is parked in her usual spot, a few spaces down from the entrance to the house. The driver's-side door is wide open, but she's not getting out.

The distant sound of shoes scuffing swiftly on pavement tears my attention from the car. Gray sweatpants and hoodie… Running down the street. He's too far away, going too fast. There's no time if…

I run to the driver's side of the car.

I can no longer feel my body. I'm dead inside, because in that instant, I know she is too.

No hope. No praying. Her body is punctured with wounds. All I can see is red. Her neck is twisted awkwardly, no longer able to support the weight of her head.

Her purse hangs from her lifeless arm. The possessions of her purse are scattered on the street.

She wouldn't let it go.

I reach for her and pull her into my arms. Her weight is too much. I fall to the ground with her. She's gone, but she's still warm. The last of her life weeps from the holes he shot through her body. For the contents of her purse.

I hold her. I can't let her go. I can't leave her when this is all we have. Seconds…

Our silence gives way to sirens in the distance. Shouts and cries of people who mean nothing to me. Because she was everything. The beginning and the end.

Then all I can hear are screams. The screams are mine, and even as they pierce the air, I know they're not enough to bring her back.

"Mom! Mom!"

ISABEL

Tristan's low, painful moans cut through the night.

The lamp is off, so the faint moonlight through the window reveals just the basic outline of his still-clothed body. We're only inches apart on the bed.

I'm afraid to move or touch him. The past several hours in Tristan's presence has taught me at least one thing. He's unpredictable. Even though he's asked for my trust, I'm not sure I can give it. Not until he proves to me that he's capable of being the Tristan I once knew. With his memory gone, I fear that's an impossible dream.

I toyed with the prospect of escape as we fell silent in the darkness hours earlier. But I thought better of a renewed attempt, and eventually sleep overtook me once more. Now, no matter what logic and self-preservation shout at me, my heart is breaking at Tristan's nightmare.

His voice belongs to the old Tristan. The boy who shared his tears and racking sobs only with me in the days after his mother's tragic death. I know the source of his pain. The thought that in consciousness he may not tugs at my growing pity for him and his situation.

To the point where I can't stay away.

I roll slowly toward him so my front is barely pressed to his side. His breathing catches, and then he stills. Unsure if he's awake and aware of me, I don't dare speak. I press my nose against the collar of his shirt. I couldn't forget that smell in a million years. The smell of Tristan in my arms, in my bed.

As his breathing evens out, I ease my arm across his torso. As soon as I'm there, his hand is wrapped over mine, tucking me tight against him. I tense at the sudden contact and then relax, melting into his warmth and unexpected affection.

"Sleep, Isabel." The command is almost tender in his sleepy rasp.

"You were dreaming."

He's silent for several seconds. "I'm awake now. Get some rest."

I lift my head from his shoulder and take in his shadowed features. Indeed, he appears fully awake now. Any vulnerability from the dream has fallen away.

I inch my palm up, resting it over his heart. Its rapid beats don't match his measured breaths or guarded expression. If only I could reach into this man and find the lover I once knew. What would it be like to escape into the deep, haunting bliss of our bodies finding perfect harmony?

His shadowed gaze offers no consolation, no promise that he'll ever be more than the kind of man who can tie me to a bed and leave me screaming for help without a second thought. Yet having him near—blood and heat and his inexplicable intensity humming against my skin, searing me despite our clothes—is both the answer to a prayer and the beginning of what I fear could become a nightmare worse than his disappearance.

I withdraw my touch and turn from him. Far enough so I can no longer feel his heat. I close my eyes and hug my pillow. Wanting anything more from him is dangerous. In less than twenty-four hours, he's simultaneously turned my world upside down and ripped me from it. I need answers. I need rest. God knows what tomorrow will bring.

The sound of the shower running wakes me. I blink against the late morning sunrays blasting through the barred window. This isn't a dream. I'm still in Mateus's home, which means Tristan is in the adjoining bathroom.

I'm furious to find that he's bound one of my wrists to the bed. I survey the room, wondering where he keeps his stash of zip ties. I kick the sheets and prepare to start screaming my head off again, when my foot touches something cool and hard on the side where Tristan slept. I grasp it with my toes enough to draw it into view. It's the pocket knife he used to release me from the ties last night. He must have forgotten about it in the moments after.

I nudge it up the bed a few inches at a time.

Water crashes in the shower, competing with the loud drumming of my heart in my ears. Every second that passes seems perilous, knowing Tristan could return before I have a chance to cut myself free.

I twist and maneuver until I can reach it. Finally I'm able to unlatch the blade. The simple act releases a shot of adrenaline to my system. The hit is so strong, I can hardly think through what I need to do next.

I'm trembling but manage to cut the thick plastic zip tie. I roll off the bed swiftly, my muscles charged and my head buzzing. With the weapon in my hand, I have options I never had before.

Tristan is only a few steps away. The man I never stopped loving. The stranger he's become.

I'm at war with his contradicting interactions with me. His unexpected tenderness mixed with his unforgiving tones and domineering behavior. But this could be my only chance to break free during daylight.

All I can do is act. Run.

I put on my shoes and grab my backpack. I quietly exit the bedroom. My heart hammers in my chest anticipating Tristan's reaction when he finds out I'm gone. Will he try to find me? Somehow I already know he will. But for how long?

The more pressing question is how the hell I'll get out of Mateus's compound. I reach the front door and remember the armed guards who manned the gates down the path. I know nothing about this place or Tristan's so-called friend, but I'm guessing leaving undetected may not be as straightforward as waltzing out the front door.

All too aware of the dwindling moments before Tristan discovers I'm missing, I venture into other rooms of the house. The foyer opens into a sitting room with several accent chairs around a coffee table. I walk along a wall of bookshelves without making a sound. I peek through a doorway into a kitchen decorated with hand-painted tiles. Karina's back is to me as she chops food facing the farthest wall.

I step back into the sitting room and consider the double doors that open to the back of the property. Carefully I slide open the door, step onto the patio, and glance around. The gardens behind the house are vast, lush, and mercifully empty of people. I move quickly, eager to reach the perimeter of the property, when a familiar voice stops me.

"Isabel. It that you?"

Panic seizes my breath. I turn my head. Mateus is coming toward me from some hidden place in the gardens. He doesn't rush. His gait is casual and comfortable, as if all of this is perfectly normal. Tristan's knife is hidden in my fist. I ready myself to use it, an anxious tremble taking over my limbs once more.

But as Mateus slows before me, his countenance is so easy and warm, I can't help but relax a little. I exhale shakily. Maybe he can help. Maybe he could be a friend...

"Isabel. Where are you running to?"

"I have to leave." I try to keep my tone even and calm. Like I'm not a prisoner on the run. Like I'm a free woman with the right to come and go as I wish. I fear I'm anything but.

He assesses me quickly, his eyes lighting on my backpack slung over my shoulder and then my closed fist.

"Where is Tristan?"

His tone doesn't change. But in his question lies another... *Does he know you're trying to leave?*

I shake my head. "Please. Just let me go."

His gaze drops again to my closed fist. "What have you got there?"

I swallow hard. I grip the knife tight again, but my palms are so slick with sweat, it slips from my grasp, rattling on the pebbled stone patio.

I curse my foible as Mateus bends to retrieve the knife. Straightening, he rolls it around in his palm, eyeing it carefully.

"Is this yours?"

I clench my jaw and lower my voice. "It's Tristan's." I pause a moment. "Can you help me leave?"

His gaze is like a tractor beam on me, full of knowing. Not unkind. A hint of compassion, maybe a touch of humor, but nothing that tells me he'll help.

"You may already know that Tristan is a very dangerous man. He's also my friend. I would never betray him."

"But he's keeping me prisoner here." I can barely contain the outrage in my voice. No one's been able to hold me against my will since… I clamp my eyes closed and reason that the emotional prison of my youth is nothing like the situation in which I now find myself.

"I keep my treasures locked away as well. You must be very important to him."

"He doesn't seem to think so."

The humor flees Mateus's features. "He does, Isabel. You are a miracle. The key—"

"To his memories. I know." I toss up my hand and try to ignore the burn of the truth.

"It hurts you," he says with a cadence that feels like a direct hit, "that he doesn't remember you."

"How could it not?"

"Do you think you can get him to remember again?"

I shrug. "I have no idea."

He gazes at me silently, as if in challenge. I've been so busy making sense of our mad dash from the city and his odd confession that I've hardly considered the possibility. Could I really make Tristan remember what he's lost? Could

I possibly have that much power?

"Isabel! Where are you?"

I jolt back at the sound of Tristan's voice bellowing through the house.

Precious seconds pass, and then he's at the sliding door. He looks around the garden but doesn't notice us right away.

"Right here, friend," Mateus says loudly but with that even quality he possesses that seems to lull one into believing everything is as it should be.

Tristan is there a moment later, and then I have two men staring at me like I've just committed a cardinal sin. Tristan is wearing only his black jeans, a dark T-shirt twisted in his fist. His skin is flushed, and his wet hair sends rivulets down his neck. A few travel down his chest, journeying across a map of scars that mar at least a dozen points on his skin. Most are white with age, ghosts of the pain inflicted upon his flesh. Some are clean and straight. Others are jagged and ugly, raised and broad from lack of proper suturing. Each one is a fresh tear in the inner fabric of my being, claiming space on the landscape of my own invisible scars.

"Tristan…" I whisper his name as heat burns behind my eyes. Who did this to him?

"What are you doing out here?" He darts his gaze over me, no doubt arriving at the same conclusions as Mateus.

I tighten my grip around the strap of my backpack and speak as calmly as my clenched jaw will allow. "You can't keep me here against my will."

Mateus's raised eyebrow answers for him. Still, my focus is on Tristan. I cling to the anger that motivated me to run.

But his scarred body has me in knots, the compass of my will spinning wildly.

Mateus offers the knife. Tristan swipes it from him and jerks his thumb toward the house.

"Inside. Now."

"Karina will have lunch for us shortly." Mateus hesitates a second. "Or perhaps you should go into town. Explore a little," he says coolly as he turns toward Tristan. "You have things to discuss, after all."

Hope springs in me at the prospect of escaping the property, even with Tristan, but his grimace dashes every ounce of it.

"We're not leaving."

Mateus squares his body with Tristan's a fraction more. "Why? Petrópolis is big enough to get lost in. You said yourself you have time."

I still at the firmness in Mateus's tone. I care less about his cryptic challenge than the fact that he's facing off with Tristan, a man he's already admitted is truly dangerous. Can Mateus set him off as easily as I seem to be able to?

"Is this your way of asking me to leave?"

"You know it isn't."

A moment of silence passes between them, and I resist the urge to back away and give the two men space.

"To capture what we most desire, sometimes we must first learn to let go," Mateus utters quietly.

Tristan is silent, his body a physical representation of his mood, rigid with frustration.

He looks at me, jerks his shirt over his head, and punches

his arms through the sleeves. He motions for my bag. "Leave your things."

I don't move. My grip tightens on the bag. My identity. Money. I'm wary to part with either under the present circumstances.

"Isabel." His sharp tone nips at the edge of my control.

I sling the bag at him in one sudden motion. "*Tristan,*" I hiss.

I pass him and return to the house, but not before catching the curl of Mateus's lips and a flicker of mischief in his eyes.

6

TRISTAN

I scan the busy street, up and down and back again, committing it all to memory. Petrópolis is vastly smaller than the metropolis we came from, but Mateus is right. It's big enough to disappear in, for a little while at least, and the Carnaval celebrations don't hurt. The people gracing the streets are raising no alarms, but I can't escape the feeling that could change at any moment.

"Are you looking for someone?" Isabel sits across from me.

We're at a little restaurant on the edge of town that Mateus recommended, but she's barely eaten. Instead, she's staring at me as if she'll find a doorway to my soul. Too bad there's no chance of that.

"I am," I say.

"Who?"

"Someone who might be here for the wrong reasons."

She sighs and leans her head to the side, as if all of this has become an exhausting game. "Who would that be?"

I look around again, seeing no one of concern. Still, I take nothing for granted. "Your guess is as good as mine."

"I doubt it. You've been acting like someone's been chasing us since we got here."

"If they aren't yet, they will be."

She glares at me, her expression falling somewhere between panic and skepticism. "Tristan, what the hell is going on? Why would you say that?"

We live such different lives. We've been sitting here less than twenty minutes, and I've already grown tired of dancing around her innocent questions. I look her square in the eye, readying myself for the real panic to set in after I say what I need to.

"Someone wants you dead."

She exhales, her breath audibly rushing past her trembling lips. "How… How can you know that?"

"The important thing is that I know. Because I do, I can make sure they don't get what they want."

She stares into her lap and grips her paper napkin tightly.

"Is it the same people who put those scars on your body?"

I shake my head slightly. I don't know where half my scars came from, but I'm certain they're not the same bad guys who want Isabel knocked off.

"Different people," I say a little softer, sensing the

heaviness of this subject might send her into an emotional fit—one I'm not especially eager to deal with in public. The last thing I need is for Isabel to make a scene.

"Why would someone want me dead?"

Her question has merit. I'm not paid to care why someone needs to be taken out, but I'm confident Isabel hasn't done anything to deserve a death wish. She's a revenge hit. Her death will send a message, maybe a warning, to someone who cares about her. If I had to guess, that person is her father.

"I'm not exactly sure why yet," I finally say.

"Then how do you know they want me dead? You're talking in riddles, Tristan."

Her voice is edging on hysterical.

"The less you know, the better. I'm only telling you so you know how dangerous it is to run from me when I'm the one trying to keep you safe. And right now, I am the *only* one who can keep you safe. Do not doubt it," I say with finality.

I run the words over in my head, convincing myself of them too. I need to keep her safe. Need to figure out a plan that will get us out of this mess alive.

Or you could skip the mess and end this now. Do your job. To hell with the past.

I wince and take another scan up and down the street.

"If that's all true, I suppose that explains why you've been so…determined." Her voice is steadier now. She juts her chin out almost defiantly. "So what happens now? We can't hide out at your friend's house forever. I have a life

THE RED LEDGER: PART 1 | 67

back in Rio. I'm sure you do too."

I stir my coffee and lift the tiny red straw to my lips. I trap the tip between my teeth and contemplate my next words.

I have a few options, most of which I'll never tell her. I could attempt to stay in Jay's good graces and do the job I was hired to do. Except now I've taken Isabel out of the city, no doubt raising suspicions about my ability to follow through. Then there's Mateus, who's become inexplicably driven to unearth the memories Isabel and I share.

"You know things…"

"About your past," she finishes the thought. "And now you expect me to be able to fill in all the blanks while we're here."

"I'm resourceful. I just need a place to start, and I can figure out most of the rest."

She swallows without making eye contact. "Why did you kiss me?"

I gnash the straw a few times. "I needed you to cooperate," I admit.

"Right. It's not like we were in love or anything." Her voice gets softer as she speaks, like she's no longer talking to me.

But her words are an invitation I'll never be able to accept. Whatever she still feels for me has to fade out. I'll never be the boy of her dreams or the lover who stars in her fantasies. The mere thought of it scares me enough to believe that stealing her away from Rio was a horrible idea.

"I'm not in love with you, Isabel."

She nods tightly and looks out the window. A few people walk into the shop on the corner. Her focus is fixed on the church across the street, though. Streaks of dirt stain the stucco below its windows. Three thin crosses mounted on the roof's round arches pierce the blue afternoon sky.

"I think this is a nightmare," she whispers.

"You have no idea," I mutter, regretting it immediately.

She looks back to me, her expression pinched with pity. Of all the things we don't know about each other, I don't have to explain my nightmares now. She was a firsthand witness to the effects of last night's horrors. God knows what I said in my sleep.

"I was with you after she died, you know."

"My mother," I mutter matter-of-factly, though I'm certain a deeper pain exists somewhere inside me.

"She was a really sweet woman. You were close. I stayed with you for a couple weeks after she died. My parents were pissed, but I didn't care. I couldn't leave you alone."

When Isabel's soul-piercing stare creeps under my skin, it's my turn to gaze at the church. The bright cerulean blue fence around it matches the sky, a vibrant distraction from the darkness of my dreams. Whoever my mother was, I know she died in my arms. If the recurring nightmare hasn't confirmed it, Isabel just did.

If these are my memories, who needs them?

"Maybe my nightmares are better than the truth. I should just be happy with an abridged version, the version my mind lets me remember."

"For what it's worth, you don't seem happy at all."

I laugh at the ridiculousness of her statement. "I'd agree with you if I had any sense of the word."

"You never feel joy."

I shake my head, feeling nothing as I do. "I survive." *I try not to get killed.*

The glimmer in her eyes seems like it might spill over into actual tears. She blinks them away rapidly and points toward the church. "I'm going over there for a few minutes, if that's okay."

My immediate response is *Hell no*, but I can't get the words out before she rises and gets several paces ahead of me. She leaves the restaurant and crosses the street to the gate that separates the building from the curb. I chase her and catch up as she reaches for the latch on the gate.

"Wait." I cover her hand with mine, trying to ignore how the smallest touch affects me.

"Wait for what?"

There's peace in her eyes. Sadness and confusion too, but under it all is a layer of stillness that I can hardly understand.

"I'm not going in there," I say firmly.

She stares steadily at me. "Are you afraid?"

I grimace, both at her question and the odd twist of emotions it inspires. Afraid? Of a church? It's all I can do to hold back the nervous laugh that wants to break free.

"No, but I'm not letting you out of my sight, which means you're not going in there."

I curl my fingers over hers, reveling in the silkiness of them as I struggle with her request. "Let's just go back—"

A door creaks loudly. "*Posso te ajudar?*"

An elderly man steps down from the entrance toward us. He's in black garb, and a string of rosaries dangles from his neck. His skin is mottled and lined with age. One eye is clouded white. Both lower when the high noon sun catches the silver circle at Isabel's neck.

"*São Paulo*," he says with a kind smile.

Isabel fingers the delicate pendant of St. Paul that rests at her clavicle. I noticed it before, briefly. Noticed it first when she was moaning my name two nights ago. When I was a reflex away from ending her life. I haven't given it much thought until now.

I can see her pulse ticking beneath the thin chain. The charm interrupts the bare beauty of the woman who wears it. Her skin shimmers like a sea of Moroccan sand. The sharp line of her collarbone slopes to her shoulder, disappearing under her shirt.

I memorize her. Desire I can't understand inspires dangerous visions. Trapping her against me in the middle of the street. Declaring war with the barriers of her clothing. Baring her. The rest of her perfect skin. Inch by inch, I unveil her in my mind. The sounds she'd make under me. The fear and desire I'd recognize with a single taste.

Something tightens in my gut at the memory of her taste. Something beyond the eagerness of her kiss. The desperation. The asking in it. No, the pure taste of her. The melding of our mouths. The familiarity of it. The way I knew her lips were mine the minute I felt them. And her tongue. The hot and greedy cavern of her perfect mouth.

I'm ready to turn the wanton cravings into truth when

her rose-colored lips curve into a soft smile for the old man. In that moment, I force myself to see her as he does. Innocent next to the likes of me. A beautiful young girl. Full of life. Clinging to faith. Hope.

"*Me chamo Antonio. Qual é o seu nome?*"

"Isabel."

He nods, rests his gaze on her for one thoughtful moment before lifting it to me.

"*E você. Qual é o seu nome?*" he says, as if I can be lured in with such a simple request.

The warmth I felt a moment ago in my visions of Isabel and all the carnal things I yearn to do to her crashes like a deluge to the ground beneath my feet, leaving me cold and sober.

I'm me again, and I have no business here.

I step away, dragging my hand away from the gate latch, disconnecting from Isabel's defiant hold on it.

"Tristan," she says. "His name is Tristan Stone."

Isabel's eyes storm when they meet mine, like some sort of mystic who knows all my darkest secrets. Or just a beautiful woman who knows my name…

ISABEL

Any fleeting comfort I felt on the doorstep of the church is swiftly ripped away when Tristan takes my hand, his grasp firm, and pulls me away from the half-blind father who would have welcomed us with open arms. I don't know what drew me there. Perhaps a moment's peace, but that's become impossible now.

I glance back at the old man, gulping down emotion I fear has no place in my current predicament. The priest draws his hand up toward the gate latch, lingering there, his eyes wide and more alert than they'd been moments ago. Tristan doesn't give him a chance. We're down the street. I'm tucked into the car seconds later. And we're off, speeding through town.

I stare at Tristan, regret and misery lodged in my throat. "Who are you?"

"No one you know." He jerks the gear shift, lurching us forward at a faster speed. "If you knew me, you'd know that's the last place I belong. And what in the *hell* were you thinking? Do you think this is a joke? Do you think there's a chance someone isn't out there right now on our scent, trying to figure out where I've taken you?"

"He's a priest. He's harmless."

"Everyone can be bought. *Everyone.* I don't care how compassionate or kind you think they are. Everyone has a price."

"You really believe that."

He stares blankly ahead. "Words to live by. It's not a hard lesson. I'd suggest you learn it before you get us killed."

I shove a hand through my already tousled hair, incensed. "Tristan, why don't you just take what you want from me and let me go home? If you don't already know who my father is, believe me when I tell you that he can protect me."

"The people who want you dead don't care about your

father's security clearances in DC."

I hesitate a moment. "If we're not safe here, then send me home."

My panic climbs with his silence.

"Tristan…"

He turns onto the dirt road that leads to Mateus's compound. My prison.

"No," he says firmly.

The rumble of the car quiets beneath the thrumming of my blood in my ears. I'm afraid and angry. And I'm suddenly aware of what might have possessed my mother when she fought with my father. Late at night when they thought I was sleeping, I would hear her words flying—a mix of language, her voice imbued with the kind of rage I could never comprehend. Then, sometimes, I'd witness her violence. From the upstairs hallway, hidden by darkness, I'd watch my father restrain her, calm her. Beyond that, he never retaliated.

Until this moment, I never believed I could be capable of such intensely negative emotions toward the man I loved. As I dig my fingernails into the car's seat, I imagine doing the unthinkable. I have to get away.

I reach for the door handle and unlatch it.

"Isabel!"

We swerve as Tristan reaches across the seat to pull me back. He slams on the brakes and eases the car onto the side of the narrow road.

"What the hell do you think you're doing?"

His proximity and anger should frighten me, but I'm

too fired up. I match his furious stare and yell, "What do you want from me?"

His nostrils flare. "For starters, I want you to stop trying to jump out of the goddamn car."

"Why do you care?"

"Because I'm trying to keep you safe." He yanks the door shut tightly and leans back, putting space between us again. "If I'd known you had a death wish, I would have kept you tied to the bed or—"

"Or what?"

"Never mind."

My heart thunders in my chest. Something in his voice changes when he talks about keeping me safe. Something that niggles at my instincts. I still love him, even if it's just the memory of him. But the more time we spend together, the less I trust the man beside me.

"What. Do. You. Want?"

He turns off the ignition, letting silence settle around us.

"Tristan—"

"My mother. Just…" He closes his eyes and swallows. "Just start there, okay? It's the most vivid memory I have."

A few minutes pass between us. Our breathing slows. Gradually, the fury between us turns into something else.

"Her name was Grace. She worked as a nurse in Baltimore. She was coming off the night shift at the hospital when it happened." I hesitate, reliving the sadness. "It was awful. The police had a couple leads but never caught the guy who did it. I often wondered if they had, if things would have been different."

He looks up at me, silently asking for more.

"You changed," I say quietly.

"How?"

I exhale slowly, taking myself back to that time. The tragedy had changed us both.

"Something went dark inside you. At first, I didn't think it would change *us*, because we were closer than ever. Unshakable. But plans we'd made began to shift little by little. When we were together, sometimes it felt like you were somewhere else. I worried that you'd never make peace with it."

"And then I left."

I nod. "We'd both applied to a few schools. I got acceptances from some Ivy League schools, so my parents were obviously breathing down my neck about that. But we both got into UCLA. It was kind of like our little escape plan. You wanted to get away from your past. I wanted to get out of DC."

"Let me guess. The plan changed."

"We were ready to send in our acceptance letters when you changed your mind. An army recruiter reached out to you right around then and started filling your head with all the possibilities."

"Then what happened?"

"I ended up staying close to home for school. I felt tethered to DC, like if I went too far I'd never see you again. Didn't end up mattering, I guess. You left for basic training. I remember you kept saying, 'I've got to do this.

It's the right thing to do.'" I close my eyes. "If you want to know the truth, I think you needed to take your revenge out on someone, and it didn't matter if it was your enemy or someone else's."

My thoughts spiral down into the agony that followed. The long months apart. The calls that came less often. Then the letter that ended everything.

Why couldn't I let him go? Why couldn't I move on and live a normal life? Have friends. Be happy. Be with someone like Kolt, who's probably wondering where I am now, along with my students and the staff at the school. I've been missing for close to twenty-four hours.

I exhale a rough sigh.

"I just couldn't let you go when there was still a sliver of hope that you'd come home. I tried to move on. I came here…"

"You came to Rio to forget me."

"I wasn't in a good place for a long time. I needed a change. Something big. Something…dangerous."

"You came to the right place."

"I suppose I did," I say, gazing out the window.

The sound of the engine revving back to life brings me back to the present. Tristan is eerily silent as he drives us back the rest of the way. We pass through the gates under the watchful eyes of the guards, climb the white stone steps of Mateus's home, and I excuse myself to get cleaned up.

I take my time in the shower, eager to let go of some of the tension and uncertainty that's taken hold of me. I towel dry my hair and put on a white sundress I packed, my thoughts tripping over our earlier conversation and his odd behavior at the church.

Maybe it'll all be worth it in the end, when Tristan can find the truth I'm still not convinced he wants to know. Maybe the people who want me dead will give up, and I can have a normal life again. *A normal life.* I didn't come to Rio to have normal. I came to shock myself out of my own malaise, brought on by missing Tristan to the point of inescapable daily pain.

I gaze up into the mirror and judge my reflection. My eyes are tired, my hair leaves much to be desired, and the dress still holds faint wrinkles from being jammed in my bag. What will Tristan see? I don't know whether to trust that our kiss was a ploy to get me to leave Rio with him. I can hardly believe that the passion crackling between us when we touch is only mine.

Venturing beyond the room Tristan and I share, I follow the sound of voices murmuring in the kitchen. I'm hit with the most amazing cooking smells, and then the sight of Karina with Mateus's arms wrapped around her waist as they whisper and laugh.

I hesitate in the doorway—hoping I can step away unnoticed—when Mateus turns to me.

"Isabel." He smiles warmly.

"Sorry. I thought Tristan might be in here."

"He's in the den. We were just getting things ready for dinner."

"It smells delicious. Can I help with anything?"

"Actually, if you could help Karina, I need to attend to

a few things."

"Go. I can finish up," Karina says, nudging him away with a coy smile.

He shoots her a heated look before leaving us alone.

Karina dices what look to be fresh chives from the garden. "Mateus says you went into town today. How was it?"

I open my mouth to speak and realize there's nothing I can say about today that doesn't sound completely crazy. I snap it shut and shrug with a smile.

She huffs out a little laugh. "I was wondering if Tristan was any different with you. I suppose not."

Her familiarity with Tristan sparks my curiosity. Karina is more than the household staff. She's obviously Mateus's lover, and she may know the new Tristan better than I do.

"You know him well?"

She sprinkles the chives into a large pot and bangs the wooden spoon on the edge a few times. "Not well. He's Mateus's friend. He doesn't pay anyone else much attention."

Even though I've just witnessed her and Mateus's embrace, a little prickle of jealousy edges its way into my thoughts. Why would she desire more of Tristan's attention?

"He doesn't seem to want many friends," I finally say.

She cocks her head. "That's probably true."

"How did he and Mateus meet?"

She shoots me a suspicious look but covers it up quickly by turning her attention to the oven.

"I don't know all the details. I don't expect I ever will. All I can say is that Mateus is in his debt. Not that he minds.

Tristan is always welcome here."

Karina pulls out a tray of nicely browned *empadas* from the oven and rests it on the granite counter. Only now do I realize how little I've eaten since leaving Rio. I'm starving, and for the first time, I feel relaxed enough to eat.

"Can I help?" I'm willing to do anything to expedite dinner or steal a bite.

Mateus returns just then. "Isabel. Come. Tristan is waiting for you."

I sigh and follow him deeper into the house until we reach the den. Tristan halts mid-pace and looks me over, his expression unreadable. I glance down and tug at the sides of my dress.

"Sorry. I didn't pack much."

He comes toward me. "You look fine."

I try not to cringe at the word *fine*. Even though it perfectly describes Tristan. Now that he's not dragging me from one place to another and I'm not trying to leap out of a moving vehicle, I can actually appreciate the physical man. His corded neck and arms that test the fibers of his black T-shirt. His narrow hips and muscular thighs. His fearless stance before me, close enough to touch.

I lift my wandering stare, only to get lost in the cool assessing eyes that have seen more than I can possibly know.

"Is everything okay?"

I swallow and pretend like I'm not blatantly checking him out, even though a little part of me still feels entitled to.

"Is black the only color in your wardrobe?"

He shrugs. "I just try to blend in."

My defenses come down a little with his honesty. "You could never blend in, Tristan."

"I do a pretty good job of it, actually."

A small smile curves my lips. "I'd find you in a crowd anywhere."

"Or on a busy street, as it were."

Thank God I found you...

As if he can hear my unspoken words, he averts his gaze. In the corner, a round, mahogany table is set for two. Several candles burn in the center. It feels oddly intimate—between the rich colors of the room, the musk of leather furniture, and the candlelight.

"Hungry?"

"Starving is more like it," I say.

Karina walks in with two steaming plates right on cue.

"Then let's eat," he says.

7

TRISTAN

Mateus arrives on Karina's heels and places two glasses of wine beside our plates. "*Saúde*," he says with a wink.

Isabel smirks as he leaves. "Why do I get the feeling he wants us to get along?"

"He likes to meddle. I had no idea how much until I brought you here."

"How long have you been friends?"

I tense at the warmth she attaches to the term. It's both foreign and uncomfortable, much like the way she makes me feel.

"Almost as long as I can remember," I finally say between bites.

Isabel is quiet for a moment. "So not long, then."

"We met a few years ago. Right after I came to Brazil.

Things were different then."

"How?"

I internally berate myself for opening the door to her question. But the more we share with one another, the less I seem to worry about the vulnerability the truth creates. Our days may be numbered. If she doesn't die by my hand, Jay's people will get to her. What does it matter what she knows?

"I was figuring out my life here. I accepted his friendship before I realized how inconvenient they could be."

"Friends?"

"Friends. Lovers. Essentially anyone who knows my name becomes a liability."

I laugh to myself at the sudden irony that, until a few hours ago, I didn't even know my own surname. I was reborn as Tristan Red the second my boots hit the ground in Rio for the first time. I have official documents with a dozen aliases, but Red is how most of the people in my world know me.

My given name is like my past. Good to know but largely irrelevant. I can never be Tristan Stone again. Isabel has to finally believe this now.

"I go by Tristan Red, by the way. I'd appreciate it if you didn't introduce me to random strangers though."

Her cheeks redden. "Sorry."

I point to her full plate. "I thought you were starving."

She exhales a deep breath and nods. We spend the next few minutes devouring Karina's masterpiece. I shouldn't feel so unguarded, but between the heavy meal and the atmosphere, I'm feeling at ease. Relaxed, even.

As we finish, she gestures to the couch and offers a hopeful smile. "Do you want to sit?"

"Sure."

Together, we move to the other side of the den where Mateus scolded me only a night ago. I refill our wineglasses, unable to stop from dwelling on the photos he showed me.

Meanwhile Isabel sits in an adjacent chair. I cross the room as she tucks her legs under her. In her flowy white dress, she's nothing short of a miracle. An impossibility.

She sips her wine and holds it on her tongue before swallowing.

"Do you like it?"

She smiles. "I do."

I sit on the couch and try not to feel like the silence is a physical thing, creeping in, beckoning me to break it and ask Isabel all the questions I should be.

"So," she says, "what should we talk about?"

Her voice is tentative, and I don't blame her after this afternoon. I should rip the Band-Aid off. Get this over with so we can both move on.

"You said my mother worked in Baltimore. If your dad works at the Pentagon, we were nowhere close. How did we meet?"

Her eyes light up. "I was your tutor."

I blink. "Excuse me?"

"I took a bus twice a week to tutor English and Spanish at an inner-city high school in Baltimore. I was trying to rack up community-service hours for my college résumé. That, and I was looking for any excuse to get out of Alexandria."

I can't hold back a laugh. "You were my tutor?"

"You were failing English before you met me," she says. "By the end of the year, you were on the honor roll."

"I suppose you think you had something to do with it."

She bites her lip with a smile. "I motivated you."

I try not to get hung up on all the ways she could have inspired my good grades. I'm guessing the eighteen-year-old version of me would have crawled across hot coals for an hour under her tutelage.

Because Isabel is more than a beautiful woman. She's fierce and kind, and I'm certain those are only a few of the layers of the person before me. She can't seem to say much without hitting a nerve, but I'm beginning to appreciate the reward. The truth. Even her dangerous affection for me is something I've found myself looking forward to experiencing during our brief time together.

"So your parents must have loved that. Falling for a boy on the wrong side of the tracks."

She traces her fingertip around the rim of her glass. "At some point, I decided to just do what I wanted. Even if it was a little scary. Even if it made my parents furious. It is my life, after all."

"It was puppy love, Isabel. Hardly worth upsetting your parents."

She narrows her eyes. "It was more than puppy love. A lot more. And it *was* worth it. Even though it nearly broke me."

I clench my jaw. We're edging into territory I'm not used to. Feelings. Heartache. Love.

"We were young," I say.

I'm not sure if I should end this now. Every exploration into my past seems to trip over the inconvenient truth that Isabel and I were once in love.

Before I can come up with a better diversion, Isabel rises from her chair and walks to me. I stare up at her as she stands before me. I can't decide if she's more angel or goddess at this moment.

"We still are young, you know."

Her knee nudges mine. Playfully, suggestively. I'm drawn to her so completely, I can't stop myself. I feather the tops of my fingers over her soft skin. The contact reverberates through me, dares me to do more, feel more.

Before I can, she leans in and sits astride me, sucking the air out of the room as our bodies meet. Her hands on my chest, her warmth covering me... I've never known this kind of temptation.

"Isabel..." I consider pushing her off but stiffen my hands into fists on either side of my thighs instead. If I keep touching her, I'll never stop.

"It wasn't that complicated, Tristan." Her voice is soothing, echoing through me like an old song. She looks into my eyes like she knows me. *Really* knows me. In ways I don't even know myself. "Boy meets girl. Boy falls for girl. Girl decides she'll break all the rules to be with the boy." Sadness hits her eyes. "Boy breaks girl's heart. Girl never recovers."

"Girl was probably better off," I whisper.

"Probably. Doesn't change the fact that I'll never be able

to love another man the way I loved you. Doesn't change the way you destroyed me, Tristan. Or that I'd do anything to feel it all again. *Anything*."

Her lips are a fraction away from mine. I attempt a sobering breath but get her essence instead. Then her lips, her taste, as our torsos and mouths melt together.

I inhale as her tongue flickers over mine. God, it's all too fucking good to resist. And her scent… Something about it hits my senses in a new way. It's familiar. Cocoa and vanilla and something else. Something I can't quite reach with my thoughts until a field of deceivingly innocent red flowers projects onto the bright-white screen of my mind.

Poppies. As far as the eye can see.

She glides one hand along my neck and into my hair, fisting gently as her body undulates above me.

I open my eyes abruptly and break the kiss. "What are you doing?"

"I'm remembering you, Tristan," she rasps against my lips.

I swear every solitary sound that comes from the woman decimates my better judgment. Even as my brain screams at me to stop this madness, I answer with a fevered kiss. Because I can't resist the way she says my name, like a siren song luring me closer to her, deeper into the sensations.

My fists ball and release a few more times before I can't fight it anymore. My fingertips meet her ankles and trail up her calves. She lifts the bottom of my T-shirt and slides her other hand up my bare chest, triggering everything else. My blood. My cock. Even my pendulum heart, racing like a fucking fool.

I close my eyes again, and suddenly we're in a dark room. Cold, save the scorching press of our bodies. She's naked, covered in shadows. Her fingernails dig into my flesh as I rock into her.

"Touch me. Tristan…please."

I can't tell if it is really her or the echo of a memory. I open my eyes and flood the vision with the golden glow of Isabel in the candlelight. Pure carnal lust drives me as I palm her knees apart, forcing her wider over me. She whimpers, and that single sound punches through the wall between reality and my hazy past. I make the final journey up her thighs, cup her ass, and haul her hard against me.

She gasps and grinds down on me, eliciting a groan that tears from my chest and rumbles inside our next kiss. It's rough and desperate. It's a flood of her perfect taste. I tease my thumbs along the edges of her panties. My head buzzes with the promise of tasting more of her… All of her. Every inch.

She's moaning my name. Clawing my bare skin and nipping at my lips like a kitten demanding affection. I'm ready to give her all I have when I hear a sound that isn't Isabel's.

Karina's figure hovers in the doorway. "Oh. I— I'm so sorry."

She disappears as quickly as she appeared, but I'm frozen, jarred by Isabel's ability to distract me so completely. Her lips are parted and swollen from my rough kisses. Her touch is no less divine, no less addictive. And deep down I know we're reliving a memory so potent I'll never be the same if I get inside her.

Against every base instinct, I draw my hands away.

"We can't do this." My voice is tight with lingering desire.

I will my palms to relish the worn leather over her silken skin. I can't feed this fantasy. I can't get this close to her.

I don't know how or when, but I feel like I've endured torture less painful than the act of pulling away from her. Gradually, I unwind, withdraw, let go...

Pushing her aside, I rise to my feet, not feeling entirely in control of myself. I'm out of breath and my body is fucking rioting. Nothing has ever felt so dangerous. I pace away and shove my hands through my hair.

"Tristan..."

Turning back, I see her flushed, perched on the edge of the couch, her dress bunched up around her thighs. An intoxicating mix of lust and anguish play on her features. Both turn me on in equal measure.

"We can't," I say firmly.

"You feel it too. I know you do."

I clench my jaw, refusing to show her how true her words are. If she knew what a single touch did to me, she'd never stop pushing for more. She'd push until I break, and I'm ready to fucking snap. This has to end. Here and now.

"You have no idea what I feel. I'm nothing more than a stranger. Do you fuck strangers, Isabel?"

She flinches like I've struck her.

"You're not a stranger. I know you…"

I take a couple steps toward her. She stiffens but doesn't recoil the way she should. She should fear me more, but I'm not sure our history will ever allow it. I stare down at her, ignoring the way my fingertips heat and prickle to touch her again.

"The Tristan you knew died years ago. He was shot full of bullets, brought back to life, and never thought about you again. I never stayed up late at night wondering what you were doing or if you were hurting. I didn't get off to thoughts of us. You were nonexistent to me. Nothing." I draw in a steeling breath that burns my lungs. "And that's never going to change."

Her cheeks bloom a deeper shade of poppy red. Her jaw falls open slightly and shuts again. Silently I beg her to believe me.

ISABEL

The muffled sound of Tristan's voice wakes me out of a restless sleep. I blink a few times. He's somewhere else in the house, probably talking to Mateus. I'm relieved and instantly heartbroken.

I went to bed alone last night, reeling from his confession. Every word cut into me like a blade. The emptiness in his eyes offered no remorse.

I mean nothing to him, and I never will. I'm the key to a locked door. A means to an end. Nothing more. All I can do is leave, lick my wounds, and wish I'd never left Rio with him. The anguish of it all has me wide awake again, despite the latent fatigue.

Morning has brightened the sky beyond my barred window. My heart sinks knowing I have to face this day. Tristan's rejection is fresh, lingering in my psyche the way his touch lingers on my skin. I kick away the sheets with a frustrated sigh, embarrassed for coming on to him in the first place. What the hell was I thinking…

I wasn't thinking. I was only feeling, reaching for magic we once had. For those few intoxicating moments, wrapped in each other, I believed we were the old us. And I was flying without a parachute, high on the way he responded to my touch, the sounds vibrating through our bodies, the familiarity of it all.

I groan and roll into my pillow. Doesn't matter if he still kissed me like he wanted to swallow me whole or touched me like he might tear me apart with the passion he felt. In the end, none of it mattered.

It never will.

I rise slowly and change into clean clothes. I look down at my bag, messy from living out of it for the past couple of days. Maybe today will be the day Tristan lets me leave. How many more memories will he pull from me before it's enough? How much deeper can he push the blade?

In the back of my mind, I think of Kolt. I miss his friendship and the way he always made me feel safe when he was near, even if I could never give him my heart. I took what I wanted and rejected the rest. I let him chase me and feel more for me than I could ever return. Worse, I disappeared without a trace...

A draining kind of discontent burdens my steps as I go down the hall toward the voices.

"We should consider leaving."

Mateus's words slow my approach outside the kitchen.

"We? You mean me?"

"No. All of us. I have a bad feeling."

"Why now? Have you heard something?" There's an edge to Tristan's voice that wasn't there before.

"You know I have eyes and ears everywhere. No signs of trouble, but—"

"Is there something you're not telling me?"

Mateus laughs nervously. "No one is ever safe, Tristan. You know that. They'll be here before we know there's trouble. I have a place a few hours south of here. We can stay there until we know more."

I hear someone shuffling around. I hold my breath and stay still. Silence. Then the sound of a coffee pot sliding out of its cradle and back again.

"You can't keep a roof over our heads forever," Tristan says.

"You need time with her."

Tristan is quiet for a moment. "I think I have all I need now."

Mateus makes an exasperated sound. "Already?"

"I can figure out the rest on my own."

"And what about Isabel?"

When Tristan falls silent again, my skin chills.

"Don't be stupid, Tristan," Mateus snaps.

"Don't be stupid? I'll probably be dead in a month. The people who want her gone won't give up. Not if we leave here. Not if we find a hundred other places to hide out. They'll want me a thousand times more than they want her for everything I know."

"And you know their tricks. You can outmaneuver them. You can keep her safe."

"Maybe," Tristan mutters. "Maybe not."

The chill morphs into a wave of sickness twisting in my gut. Someone wants me dead. And the love of my life doesn't even care.

"Karina saw you together last night," Mateus finally says.

"I know."

My cheeks heat, knowing we'd been caught.

"You care for her."

"I want to *fuck* her. It's animal attraction. Nothing more. And last night was a mistake I have no intention of repeating. I was relieved that Karina interrupted us. I can't seem to…"

"What?"

"Nothing." Tristan's voice is barely audible.

My heart starts to race. Last night's humiliation feels even more raw now. I should go before they find me eavesdropping on their conversation. But Mateus's sense of urgency has me planted where I stand, desperate to learn more and find out our next steps.

"Do what you wish. You know what I think. Be ready

at noon if you want to come with us."

I don't wait to hear more. I retreat to the bedroom. My thoughts sprint through what I need to do. Pack what little I have. Find Tristan or appeal to Mateus. Maybe he'll take me with him. I can't trust Tristan's heart.

I throw my toiletries in my bag with the few clothes I brought. The sound of a vehicle rolling over the gravel in the front drive draws my attention up. I glance through the window as a black Hummer idles near the gate. The armed guard is speaking to the driver obscured behind the vehicle's tinted windows, but I can't hear what they're saying.

Then the guard's head jerks back violently with a sharp pop, and he collapses onto the ground. I slap my hand over my mouth to mask my scream at the sight of his wound gushing onto the chalky white stones.

The second guard lifts his automatic weapon and gets a few shots off before he's given the same fate—a single answering crack of the air that sends his gun and limbs flailing. He drops like a ragdoll to the ground only a few feet away from his post. My shaking hand closes tightly around my pendant. I try to scream, but I'm frozen in place until the Hummer lurches into motion toward the house.

"Tristan. Tristan!"

I grab my bag and run to the kitchen to find him, but he's gone.

"Tristan!"

I spin around and run into the sitting room, finding it empty too. I scream his name again, unable to control the violent shaking of my limbs. Finally the back door opens and Tristan is there, his eyes wide with concern.

"What's wrong?"

"They're here. They killed them. The guards. They're dead. Oh my God, Tristan. They just shot them both."

He grabs me by the arms. His eyes turn from blue silver to dark steel. "Who? Who shot them?"

I can only shake my head and swallow over my tears. "I don't know," I whisper. "But I think they're coming for us."

Mateus rushes into the room, eyes wide.

Tristan looks up. "We have to go. Right now. Get Karina."

Mateus exhales in a rush. "She's gone… She went into town to get a few things before we left."

Tristan hesitates. Precious seconds pass as he quietly assesses the other man. "Who the fuck did you tell?"

Mateus pales. "No one, Tristan. I would never put you in danger. Not after what you did for me."

Tristan pulls a gun out of his waistband and points it square at him, shoving me to the side. "You're lying. I know the price on her head. What's mine?"

Mateus takes a tentative step forward, halting when Tristan cocks the gun. My heart lodges in my throat.

Mateus speaks quietly. "That's not what happened. You have to trust me. I would never betray you."

"I don't trust anyone, and you know it."

Mateus lifts his hands in surrender. "Money will never turn my alliances. I have no reason to bring harm on you."

Tristan's jaw is tight. "No? Getting rid of me wipes the debt. And it's a pretty big fucking debt, if I recall."

Mateus doesn't move. His expression is steady. "A debt you've never called, friend."

I jolt at the sound of two car doors slamming in close succession, but neither men flinch. Voices outside. Footsteps on stone. Then I can only hear my own heartbeat pumping blood and adrenaline through my veins. My throat tightens with panic. I don't know who to trust, but the bad guys who want at least two of us dead are mere seconds away.

"Tristan. We need to get out of here."

"She's right," Mateus says evenly. "If your comrades make it through the front door, none of it will matter. They'll kill us all."

Comrades?

What the hell has Tristan gotten us into? The phantom demons he's been talking about have suddenly become real. If I thought I was living a nightmare before, I'm certain I've just arrived at the gates of hell.

Tristan grimaces tightly. "Where's the car?"

"Downstairs. Keys are in the ignition."

Tristan gestures with the tip of his gun toward the hallway. "Let's go. Move."

I manage a relieved exhale as we move together through the house. Tristan pauses at a second bedroom, where he retrieves his bag and slings it over his shoulder.

"This way." Mateus opens the door to a basement stairway that leads us to a dark and dingy garage.

In it sits a cream-colored classic car that looks like it's decades old but in mint condition.

"You're kidding me," Tristan says.

"It's fast," Mateus assures him, slipping into the driver's seat.

Tristan tugs my backpack off.

"No, I need this," I say, my voice trembling badly.

"I know you do. But you need to go with Mateus." He rounds to the back of the car, pops the hatchback open and, after a few seconds, closes my backpack in it, slinging his own bag over his shoulder again.

"What are you going to do?" I ask shakily.

My breathing is ragged as he walks toward me. I feel like I could pass out. When my fingers start tingling, I worry that I might. Tristan seems eerily calm, though.

"I'm going to stay here and take care of this," he says.

I shake my head violently. "No. Come with us. You have to get out of here. They'll kill you."

"Not if I have anything to say about it. I'll meet you after."

Mateus looks up at us through the rolled-down window. "There's a safe house in town where we can stay until the coast is clear. It's near—"

"Fuck your safe house." Tristan's anger breaks his calm but eases when he looks back to me.

My brain whirls and stutters until it lands on at least one place I'd rather be than here under siege.

"I know a place," I say quickly.

Tristan stills, his gaze locked to mine.

"From yesterday." I touch below my right eye, hoping he picks up the hint.

He nods slightly and looks down at Mateus. "Drop her

at the edge of town. She knows the rest of the way." Then he curves his hand firmly at my nape, forcing me closer. His voice drops to a whisper. "Don't let him follow you. And don't fucking talk to anyone. Blend in. Understand? I'll meet you there."

"Okay." I can barely get out the next words. "What if something happens to you?"

I can't lose you again...

"I put your phone and some money in your backpack. Get out of Brazil as fast as you can. If you can't talk your way out of it, don't be afraid to get creative. Bribes always help."

My eyes threaten to bulge out of their sockets when he presses the gun into my hand. "Take this. Feel free to shoot him if you need to."

"Tristan, I can't."

"You do what you want, remember? You're braver than you realize." His hands fall away. "One more thing. It's important."

"What?"

His expression hardens. "There's a red notebook in your bag. If I don't come back, give it to your father. No one else."

Another bang sounds from upstairs. My heart nearly flies out of my chest.

"Now get the fuck out of here."

He steps away, and I rush on shaking legs to the passenger side, joining Mateus in the car. He starts the engine and rests his hand on the gear shift.

"Mateus."

He looks up through the window. Tristan simultaneously leans in.

"If anything happens to her—"

"I know, Tristan. Trust me...I know." Mateus looks away, presses the garage opener, and stares ahead. "Take care of yourself, my friend."

8

TRISTAN

I pull a second handgun out of my bag and peek under the door as it opens. Mateus can nearly clear the opening with the Envemo as I catch movement by the Hummer. Then a man in black whips around the back of it and aims for the windshield. My heart slams against my chest as I get a shot off. He drops limp to the ground.

Mateus peels out, barely missing the body. I watch only long enough to see them speed down the road before I turn back for the house, every sense on high alert. This is nothing like a hit, but nothing I can't handle. Sometimes it's complicated. Of course, that was before Isabel. Before I signed myself up for a lifetime of ducking extinction—mine and hers.

Jay had messaged me twice this morning asking about

Isabel. I should have known it was a warning shot. Maybe Mateus's gut was right, or maybe he just offered me to Jay's backup plan on a silver platter. I hoped it wasn't the latter, since he was Isabel's only chance to get out of this bullshit alive.

"Red!"

The hairs stand up on the back of my neck because I know the voice booming through the house.

"Come on, Red. Where's the girl? I know she's pretty, but you gotta give her up now."

I move up the stairs without a sound, sliding my back along the wall as I go. All the while, I'm cursing Jay. Of all the people to send…

I make it to the hallway and move toward the sound of his loud footfalls. He's still a big fucker.

"Boss isn't happy," he calls out. "But we can figure this out, man. We just need the girl so we can get this done."

I round the corner and find him in the foyer, pacing casually. I aim for the back of his crew cut when he turns. His face splits with a crooked smile.

"There you are," he says, making no effort to draw his weapon.

"Crow. Long time, no see."

He chuckles. "Yeah. I'm hard to miss too."

He lowers his big frame onto the edge of one of the accent chairs. I'm surprised it doesn't tip under his weight. Crow fits his name. Black hair and black eyes and, if I had to guess, a black heart to match. Big and loud and there's no vermin too indecent to fatten his wallet. Not that I'm one to judge, except he has a penchant for pissing in my backyard from time to time.

"Jay's wondering what you've been up to. Your trigger finger broken?"

"Not remotely," I mutter, my aim more than steady.

I'm ready to push Crow for more information when I spot movement in my periphery. I knew he wouldn't be alone. The third party is stone-faced and leaner than both of us, edging his way into view from his hiding spot in the entryway. His eyes are round and glassy, like an owl who sees everything. I'm not sure he's blinked since I noticed him.

"Drop it." His voice wavers.

"Have you met Hogan? No?"

Crow lets out a shitty, condescending laugh. Despite it, I decide to play nice and let the gun fall with a thud on Mateus's expensive Persian rug. Thankfully I don't need it to fuck Crow up and take out his helper. Crow's overconfidence has gotten him into trouble before, and I'm more than ready to take advantage of it. Just as soon as I find out a few things.

"How did you find us?"

Crow draws his gun and points lazily to the chair. "Have a seat."

"No thanks."

He grins. "I insist."

I sit as he grabs his phone and talks into it walkie-talkie style. "Otto, we have him upstairs." Silence and a few crackles. "Otto."

Crow's distracted and he's about to get bad news, but I'm more worried about Hogan on my right, who's either sleep-deprived or high as a kite.

"She's gone," I say. "So is Otto."

Crow's expression melts into a displeased snarl. He straightens and comes closer to stand directly in front of me. "Where. Is. She?"

"Couldn't say."

He crosses his arms and stares down at me, no doubt enjoying his perceived position of power. "What happened, man? You had to hit it a few times before you put a bullet in her? That's some weak shit."

"Not sure it's any of your business."

"Kind of my business now, don't you think? Where's she going?"

"Probably driving back to Rio right now. You know who she is. Feds are probably hot on this and working with the police to find her and get her back home."

His eyebrows jerk upwards. "Feds? You've got a red dot on your fucking head, and you're sending her home to Daddy? What the fuck for? You in love with her or something?" He pauses a beat. "Aren't the Feds the ones who tried taking you out to begin with?"

I hate that Crow knows anything about me at all. But we all come from somewhere. I was a special ops mission gone wrong. Crow's mob boss family created a protégé killing machine who made better bank on private assignments than TVs falling off trucks.

"If you found us, so can they."

"I've been tracking you for days, Red. Didn't get the go-ahead from Jay to move on you until this morning, otherwise you'd have seen me the day after you *didn't* pop the girl." He shakes his head. "This was easy money too. I don't get it."

He knows better than to question my ability. He's right. Killing Isabel would have been an easy hit. Controversial maybe, but hardly a challenge in execution.

He leans closer, bracing himself on the chair's arms. It's a precarious position for him if not for the all-seeing eye a few feet away. Crow knows this, so he's being cocky. He's daring me to make a move. Under normal circumstances, I would. I'm not afraid of getting shot. I'm not sure I'm afraid of dying either. What scares me now is the prospect of leaving Isabel unprotected. Because once Mateus drops her off, she will be.

I curse inwardly, harnessing some calm. "Why is she so important?"

"We're not paid to ask questions, Red. Point and shoot. Don't get killed. You know the drill."

"Maybe she's worth more than the price on her head."

He cocks an eyebrow. "Worth more alive? Doubtful."

I shrug. "Suit yourself."

He hesitates, but I know he's got money-hungry running through his veins.

"More than the cost of getting put on Jay's naughty list?"

I offer him a million-dollar smile, hoping he takes the bait. "Why don't we have a drink? I'll tell you what I know."

He laughs and straightens. "Sure, why not. What's the rush?" He walks toward the bar and looks toward his comrade. "Want something?"

Hogan lowers his gun and nods. Junkie. He'll catch any high he can, even if it means taking his eyes off me.

"If he gets out of that chair, shoot him," Crow barks as he pulls two glasses down from the bar.

I laugh to myself. Crow's cocky, but he's not stupid. Most men who turn their backs to me end up dead.

I stare down the barrel of the gun trained on me when another face appears over his shoulder. Karina steps into the house.

No. I feel the blood drain from my face.

I don't have time to rethink Mateus's betrayal, because if Karina dies like this because of me, he'll never forgive me. The junkie swivels, turning his back to me. In a fraction of a second, I lift from the chair and map my steps toward her, already knowing I won't reach her in time.

Then her face changes into something wild, and I see the gun. She lifts it and fires, sending an explosion of blood out the back of the man. His gun swings limp around his finger as he brings his other hand to what's left of his neck.

I dive for my gun and turn it to Crow, but he's ducked out of the room.

I fire randomly down the hallway, where he's likely waiting for his opportunity to fire back, as I make my way to Karina.

She's still wild-eyed and shaking, clutching the gun tightly in her hands.

"Nice shot," I say in a hushed tone.

"I was aiming higher."

My mirth fades when a bullet whizzes by, narrowly missing me and shattering one of the paintings on the wall. I duck farther into the entryway, feeling less than safe behind a few layers of drywall.

I push Karina over the threshold. "Get out of here. Mateus went into town. He'll find you. Go now."

She doesn't acknowledge me, but she obeys, disappearing out the door. I slam it shut and peek around the corner for any signs of Crow. I have a vantage of the empty hallway, and the huge shadow spilling out from one of the extra bedrooms tips me off. Two down, one to go.

"How's this going down, Crow?"

"You tell me. I thought we were talking."

I can hear him reloading.

"Tell Jay I got away with the girl. I'll loop you in after we get out of the country."

"Like hell you will. This is a death wish and you know it," he shouts.

"Your loss."

Silence falls on the house.

"How much?"

I bend and grab the dead man's gun, tucking it into my waistband.

"This is your last chance to pique my interest, Red. Then I'm coming for you and it's fucking over. Tell me how much she's worth."

"Everything," I grit out, knowing the sound will never reach him. I leave the entryway and move silently down the hall, gun raised and ready.

The pendulum swings in slow motion.

I shoot the first thing I see.

"Fucker!"

I turn the corner into the bedroom, and he's pushing back by his heels, cradling his bloody hand against his stomach. He only hesitates a second before he raises his left and begins firing, nearly emptying the chamber.

I hiss as one drills through my upper arm. I duck back into the hallway and curse under my breath.

"You left-handed?" I push hard on the wound that's already saturating my shirt with blood.

"I am now, you piece of shit. Show me your face, and we'll finish this."

I clench my teeth against the pain, but something in me doesn't want this to end the way Crow thinks it will. I need to get back to Isabel, but I need to send a message too.

"Seems like a waste, doesn't it?"

Crow answers with a barrage of gunfire through the doorway, punching through the drywall near me. I scramble down the hallway. Mateus's master bedroom is a dead end.

Hurriedly I cinch a handkerchief on the bureau around my upper arm. I'm not overly concerned about the wound, but I'd rather not pass out before I have a chance to send Crow back to his maker if I need to.

Between his lumbering steps, I hear him crash into the wall before continuing down the hall toward me. How he sneaks up on anyone I'll never know. I do know I'm at an advantage, though. Crow has one good arm and only a couple of shots left. I decide to give him a target and hope he wastes them. I pivot into the doorway and aim for his shoulder. *Crack crack.* I duck and dodge his answering shots, the last he has, but his steps don't slow. He turns into the bedroom, his eyes wild with murderous rage. I hit my mark, but the gushing from his shoulder doesn't seem to faze him at all.

He advances on me. Goddamnit, I didn't want to kill Crow. I back up and ready myself to put his name on the list that's already too long.

"Do you want to die, or do you want to help me send a message?"

"I'm gonna tear you limb from limb. There's no talking your way out of it."

"You're the one with the dot on your head now, so I'd suggest you reconsider."

"That's not how this works."

"I'm not playing by the rules anymore if you haven't figured that out already."

He keeps coming at me, arms wide like a blood-thirsty gorilla. *Fuck fuck fuck.* I aim for his knee and fire.

He cries out and his leg buckles, sending him to the floor. Injured or not, he's enormous. I might be faster and smarter, but he's stronger. So I move fast. I strike him with the butt of my gun and use his break in balance to shove him to the ground, belly down. He grunts when I wrench his arm behind him, exacerbating the pain where the bullets are still lodged in his thick shoulder muscles.

"Time to finish our little chat," I say, pressing the gun barrel to his temple.

"Fuck you," he wheezes.

I change the angle of the gun, adding pressure so he feels the fear of the inevitable. "Last call, Crow."

He exhales roughly a few times. "What's it matter? Jay's gonna kill me after this anyway."

"I don't have time to listen to you wrestle with your mortality, Crow. *Last call.*"

He gnashes his teeth and curses again with less force.

I take that as surrender.

"This is mercy," I say.

"I don't want your fucking mercy!"

I reposition my knee above his bloodied hand and add pressure. He shudders from the pain.

I lean in and lower my voice. "Listen carefully. They're going to find you here eventually, and you're going to relay a little message for me. Tell Jay to forget my name. Tell her to forget the girl. Because if she doesn't, everyone she sends for me is going to wish for the mercy I'm showing you right now."

He huffs in and out, his breathing labored. Even as the vow violates everything about the way I've lived these past few years, I know it's true. I can't let these bastards have her. The worst thing she ever did was fall in love with me, and that's not a reason to die.

"Who is she to you?"

"All you need to know is that she's mine, and I'm not backing down."

I leave Crow hogtied in Mateus's bedroom. On my way to hijack the Hummer for my ride back to town, I see Karina's red sedan idling up the road. I jog toward it, praying to hell there wasn't a fourth member of Crow's crew who could have gotten to her. Relief floods me when the driver's door swings open and she emerges.

"Karina. What are you doing here?"

"Get in. Hurry. Mateus is waiting for us."

Not wanting to waste time, I get in and she hits the gas, jolting us forward. A few minutes later, we're at the edge of town. The streets are busy with a weekend market. Lots of eyes, but lots of opportunities to go unnoticed too.

I see Mateus leaned against his car as Karina parks nearby. He doesn't pay me a second glance. He goes to Karina and all but rips her out of the car and hauls her into his arms. "Karina," he whispers into her wavy black hair.

I glance back to the crowd, scanning it for the one familiar face I'm eager to find.

"Where's Isabel?"

Mateus looks up, his forehead creased with worry. "I did as you asked, Tristan. I would have kept her with me otherwise."

"It's fine," I say, though I'm sure an apology is in order since I strongly considered killing him not so long ago. My distrust of him could have cost Isabel her life, a possibility that won't be ruled out until I find her safe.

I reach into my bag. He tenses until I retrieve the frame.

"Here," I say, handing it to him. "You probably won't be able to go back for a while. I figured you'd want this."

He takes it without a word, opens and closes it quickly. Then he looks up and slowly reaches out his hand. I pause to consider the gesture and what it means. A reaffirmation of a relationship built on blood and revenge. Then I lift my arm and our palms meet and mold.

It's as close to forgiveness as we'll get for now.

"Where will you go now?" he asks.

I glance back to the crowd. "Time to disappear."

He takes the keys from Karina and hands them to me. "For your getaway."

"Thanks," I say.

"Thank you for not shooting me."

Karina's eyes grow wide and angry. "What? You were going to shoot him?"

Mateus hushes her. "It's nothing. I promise you."

"It's nothing? He is your friend, Mateus."

His lips thin. "He is," he says quietly. He reaches for the door of the Envemo and ushers Karina inside.

9

ISABEL

The air, weighted with three hundred years of desperate prayer, smells of old wood and the soot of scented candles. The heavily painted figure of the Messiah stands at the center of the church, silent and still, offering his open arms to the devout. The needy. The desperate.

The half-blind priest bolts the front door and gestures to the back of the church. "*Me siga.*"

I offer him a weak smile, ready to follow him to the only place I thought to hide when Tristan sent me off. With no hesitation, Padre Antonio agreed to give us shelter here tonight. He asked for nothing in return. Even as I am growing to distrust nearly everyone, I have faith in his genuine kindness.

Seeming to sense my somber mood, he pauses and

touches my arm gently. His skin is dry and warm to the touch. The simple kindness wraps around me, threatening to unravel my quickly fraying emotions. I blink back tears.

He hushes me and speaks softly in Portuguese. "Rest here, Isabel. Come back when you are ready." Without another word, he walks away, leaving me alone with my thoughts in the empty hall.

I haven't stepped foot in a place of worship for years. Not since Grace's funeral. My parents all but turned their backs on Tristan's tragedy, and in turn, I turned my back on the traditions of our faith.

Still, something faint rings inside me. I can't remember a time when I've needed hope more.

Careful not to disturb the silence, I move up the narrow aisle. Whatever drew me to the church gate yesterday with Tristan on my heels compels me now into the pew and onto my knees. I lean forward, anxiety tight in my belly. The lacquered wood is warm under my palms and against my forehead. A small comfort. I exhale heavily, racked with worry and fatigue.

This unexpected journey with Tristan, fighting for our lives and more, has turned me inside out. It's made me raw and weak and aimless. Yet even as I long for the safety and security I took for granted every day before, I can't deny wanting to save Tristan from this nightmare too. I have no idea how I can, though. I've never felt more powerless in my life, flung from place to place, kept in the dark by the lover of my past.

How can the broken man I still care for beyond reason

be the one to save me? Can he even save himself?

I'm miles from Tristan, but I pray he hears me.

Please.

Please come back to me. Please live.

Please fight for us… Survive for us… Remember us…

Over and over, I whisper my deepest pleas. All the while, visions of the horrific acts I witnessed earlier consume me. I grip the back of the pew tightly, refusing to believe the same fate could come upon Tristan. He's too strong. Too determined. Too broken to let them win…

I squeeze my eyes against tears. He's not dead. I'd feel it if he were. I'd know. There'd be an earthquake in my soul. Some kind of sign.

I look up at the cartoonish figure before me. No change in his peaceful countenance. I don't bow my head again, because this is no longer a quiet prayer. I'm as desperate now as all the troubled, poor, and sick souls who've passed through these doors and bruised their knees on the crude floor.

"Help me save him," I utter amidst the quiet crackle of candles. "Tell me what to do."

A door slams in the back. I grip the pew with knuckle-whitening force. My heart stutters and then launches into wild beats. Then I hear his voice mingled with the priest's.

"Tristan."

I scramble to my feet as he appears from the hallway. He's disheveled and dirty and bloody, but sweet mercy, he's alive.

I run toward him and throw my arms around him.

"You're alive." The word tears like a sob from my throat.

"You're safe," he whispers against my hair, holding me almost painfully tight against him.

I mold myself to him as if the surface of my body needs proof of his existence. The more we touch, the more real this is. He catches me closer still.

Only then do I remember the barriers that still exist between us. The reality that came between us last time we were this close. I untangle from our embrace and take a small step back.

"Sorry. I just… I thought you were dead. I was so scared."

"Not today."

His hands fall to his sides. Then I realize the blood he's covered in is his own. A strip of cloth is wound tightly around his upper arm, seeping red and wet. I blink rapidly over my tears and swallow down all the emotion that wants to bubble up.

"You're hurt."

"It's okay. It's nothing."

"Nothing? You're bleeding, Tristan. You need a doctor."

He laughs lightly. "Hardly. I should clean it though."

I take his hand and lead him back down the hallway to the room the priest promised was ours for the night. The back of the church consists of a desk in the corner, several wooden shelves with old musty books, and a small twin bed that seems freshly made. Before I can ask for cleaning supplies, Antonio emerges from a tiny bathroom with a bowl of water, gauze, and disinfectant gathered up in his arms.

I rush to him. "Here. Let me help you."

I take the supplies and lay them out on the desk with shaking hands.

"He is your friend?" He speaks in a hushed tone that only I can hear.

His expression is pinched with concern. I can't imagine how this looks to him. He must know we're in trouble—or that Tristan is. I glance back to Tristan, who is looking out the windows.

"He's a friend, yes. Thank you for everything," I answer quietly.

"Here." Tristan comes closer, reaching into his bag with his wounded arm and withdrawing a brick of *reals*.

The father steps back like the offering might burn him. "No, no."

"Tristan, he doesn't want it. Come sit so I can dress your wound."

Tristan stares at the old man, his gaze stoic. "No one can know we're here. Do you understand?" His Portuguese is heavily nuanced with his American accent.

The father waves his hand again and shakes his head. "You are safe here. I can assure you. I will leave you now. I will bring you food in the morning. Yes?"

Tristan's frown deepens, but I step between them and place a hand on the priest's shoulder.

"Thank you. We are so grateful."

The old man offers me an uneasy smile. Tristan makes him nervous, but I'm beginning to understand why. This is life and death now.

"I will come check on you in the morning," Antonio says before shuffling out, leaving us alone once more.

"I should have had you give it to him." Tristan drops the money onto the desk and tugs his T-shirt over his head, leaving only the bloody dressing on his arm.

"He doesn't need a bribe. He only wants to help."

"We'll see," he mutters. "Are you sure you can handle this?" He glances down and slowly begins unwrapping the dressing.

I swallow hard. Blood has never made me squeamish, but seeing Tristan hurt seems to trigger physical pain of my own. I feel it on the surface of my skin, a painful prickling in my fingertips.

"If you're not going to see a doctor and get this taken care of properly, then I don't suppose I have much choice."

"You know why we can't."

"I know," I say, resigned to these new circumstances by which we're bound. I recognize we're in a space where life and death supersede creature comforts. Like a hospital. A hotel. A home.

I collect a cloth and dip it into the warm water. Carefully I work to get the wound clean, hoping to minimize Tristan's discomfort, though he seems barely affected.

"That looks better."

"Told you it'd be fine. Just grazed me."

I roll my eyes, because even though the damage is clean and less gory, the bullet that "grazed" him took a long trail of flesh with it. Even now, I can see it'll be another scar that no amount of care can prevent. Yet nothing about this seems to give Tristan pause.

"Who were those men, Tristan? Why did Mateus call them your comrades?"

He gazes toward the ceiling as I dab antiseptic on the wound. He doesn't flinch or speak.

"I don't understand why they want me dead. What could I have done to bring all this on?"

"I'm guessing you didn't do anything. But sometimes innocent people can get caught in the crossfire if they're standing too close to the bad guys."

He washes his hands and face in the bowl. I place a fresh bandage on his arm as he does, satisfied that the gash is protected for now.

"Your father is obviously connected," he continues. "Is there anyone else close to you who could be in trouble?"

I frown. "My father has a desk job. He's not out in the field."

"That doesn't mean anything. He can piss people off from his desk. You have no idea what kind of situations he could be involved with."

I press my lips tightly together. What Tristan's saying could be true. My father could never talk much about his work due to the confidential nature of it. I grew up knowing this, but nothing about his nine-to-five routine ever bled into our home life to make me think he was into bad things. Certainly nothing akin to the hell I've experienced today.

"It's been a long day." Tristan's tone betrays his fatigue.

His eyes are tired but still vibrant. Full of life and the glimmer of determination I recognized as he sent me off with Mateus. He seemed different then. Less heartless captor. More...*Tristan*.

He sighs and runs his fingertips over my hands, taking them into his. "What would you have done...if I didn't come back?"

I worry the inside of my lip and try to maintain a brave face, but the possibility of losing him all over again is too fresh. Never mind how I may not have been able to escape with my life when a vehicle full of men with guns were on the hunt for me.

I look away, not trusting myself not to break my composure. "Honestly, I don't know."

He pushes my hair over my shoulder, his touch unexpectedly tender. "Me neither," he says softly.

He weaves his fingers into my hair and drags them gently over my scalp and down my neck. I close my eyes at the sheer relief of his touch. I hear the rough slide of his body coming off the desk, feel the warmth of his proximity. We're so close that his masculine and earthy scent hits my senses.

When he leans in, I can feel his breath and then the tip of his nose across my cheek. I'm trembling, uncertain if I can handle the sensations his closeness brings. When his lips trail my jaw, my breath hitches.

"Tristan... What are you doing?"

He skims his hands down my arms, splays his palms across my back, and brings me tighter and closer against him.

"I'm remembering you."

He spins us and lifts me onto the desk, spreading my legs to take the space between them. He steals my next sharp intake of breath with a rough kiss. That quickly, he's all over my senses. His hands are everywhere, and so are mine. Raking over his broad shoulders, kissing his jagged scars with my fingertips, reclaiming him, one inch at a time.

His stubble scrapes my lips. "Can't stop. Not this time."

"No." God, if he stops now, I'll never survive.

I've been held on the brink for far too long. Starved of Tristan and all the things his touch once inspired. Passion on my skin. Faith in my heart. A future with him in it.

He pulls my shirt over my head and leans in quickly to reclaim my mouth. The kiss is almost bruising in its intensity, but I revel in it. I unhook my bra, let it fall to the floor, and hoist myself closer so our bare chests meet. Close enough to feel the tick-tock rhythm of his heart.

Our exploring touches fill the minutes. My ragged breaths turn to whimpers. Where I was tentative before, I'm frantic now. I press my nails into his flesh, silently begging for more.

He palms my breasts, squeezing and stroking the tender tips until I'm pulsing with desire.

"I need to taste you." He tucks his hand under the waistband of my shorts, new heat in his eyes.

How many times had I fantasized about this moment since he left? Those words on his lips, that promise lingering in the air between us?

I nod breathlessly, my lips tingling and my skin on fire. Inch by inch, he draws my shorts down my thighs, baring me completely.

Then his lips are soft and slow, leaving a wet trail over my breasts, down my belly, and over the tiny jewel at my navel, almost all the way to the place where I throb for him.

His next touch is featherlight as he opens me under his hungry gaze. He's fixated on the space between us. I whimper when he bends, and his exhale barely kisses my flesh. I curl my hands over the edge of the desk. I'm afraid to move another inch, lest he change his mind and leave me this way, so vulnerable and needy.

But he doesn't back away. He leans in, nudges me wider with his broad shoulders, and consumes my flesh with his mouth. The delicious contact pulls another helpless cry from my lips.

"Do you have any idea what this does to me, Isabel? Being this close to you. Tasting you. Knowing the sounds you make…"

He pauses only a moment before coming at me again. Tasting and taking and tormenting with every wicked lash of his tongue. The more he gives me, the more I need. I'm greedy, ravenous for as much of him as he'll offer. As if his instincts are linked to mine, he licks me harder, grips me tighter. I fist his hair and struggle to keep up with the sharp incline of sensation.

I'm so close, my hips lifting into his ministrations, when he straightens abruptly. He curves his hand behind my neck and brings us together. "I want the rest of you." The sound is gritty and molten. Rock and fire.

I reach for the button of his jeans and wrap my legs

around his narrow hips.

He kisses me hard, flooding my mouth with the taste of me and this unhinged lust we're drowning in. He presses his erection against my sex.

"Isabel…" He cups my cheek, forcing my stare to his. "It's not going to be the same. You need to know that."

A few heavy seconds pass between us. I believe him and I don't. I care, and the next second, I'm convinced I don't. I shake my head as much as his grip on me will allow. "I don't care."

His eyes darken with lust and restraint I'm not sure he'll be able to maintain. Yet he holds back, seemingly unable to take us further. Why?

Because this is more than our two bodies seeking sexual relief. This is my war-torn heart colliding with the reality of our present turmoil. No matter how hard I pray, I'll never have the Tristan I fell in love with. The man before me—the one who took the slice of a bullet fighting off those men today—is the only one I'll ever know again.

I exhale a shaky breath, drag my gaze down his scarred chest and back to his haunted eyes. "I'm not the same. I've changed too."

Maybe not on the outside. Maybe not in the ways that matter to a man like Tristan. But at this moment, we're matched in our intensity. In our brokenness. We're both empty and unwilling to survive another minute without being filled. What's this life if we can't fill the emptiness with each other?

I reach for him, but he takes my arm and shifts me off

the desk. His next kiss is different. Sweet and savage. Tender and unapologetic. As if he's already asking permission for what will happen next. Turning me swiftly to face the table, he holds my wrist behind my back.

His breath is warm at my ear. "Like this."

I inhale a quick breath to feed the adrenaline spike he's inspired. I nod. And then I can feel him guiding my legs apart, pushing inside me, filling me. I tense and release, surrendering to the breathtaking feeling. I moan and let my head fall back against his shoulder. He's a wall of muscle behind me, every inch of his strength governed by the act of consuming the space between us and intimately joining us.

He releases my arm and bands my hips so I feel every inch of his next thrusts.

I slap my hands on the desk, using its steadiness for leverage. A wild heat races across my skin, but the fire burning on the inside is raging, consuming the last of my inhibitions. Obliterating the fear. Calling back memories I've kept at a distance for too long.

His free hand roams my flesh, plucking at my breast and then tormenting the place his mouth abandoned with a series of strokes over my clit that inspire even more primal sounds from me. I surrender to his rugged pace and race toward the firestorm of the orgasm I know is coming.

"Tristan… Tristan… *Tristan*."

Every iteration of his name on my lips is louder, heavier, matching his drives. The sound is both demand for more and dedication to the climb that isn't even bliss. It's air. It's blood. It's us. Whatever is left of us now…

That truth sinks into my skin, melting into the places that Tristan has already set on fire until there's no place else to go.

His tortured groan, his teeth bared and sinking into my shoulder, and the clawing need to release... Everything comes together to push me over.

"Tristan!"

I scream it until he slaps his hand over my mouth, buries himself to the hilt, and muffles the pinnacle moment until I'm wilted and reduced to a series of long, delirious moans into his hot palm.

We collapse together. Me over the desk. He against my back. He surprises me by pushing deeper still. I gasp, and he sighs with such audible satisfaction that my heart squeezes in my chest.

Already I know I need this to mean more to him.

I've changed, but I'm wired to love Tristan. My love for him will never stop seeking its reflection. Until he says it again, I'll survive on those little sounds and the glints of affection in his eyes before they darken with truth I've yet to truly understand.

The warm night and our passion cool on our skin. Tristan lifts, and I turn to see him walking away toward the bathroom, zipping himself away. He returns with a warm cloth and offers it to me.

"Sorry, I—"

"It's fine. I have it covered." I take the cloth with a shaky hand.

His brows come together a second before he turns

away again. He riffles through his bag for another T-shirt as I attempt to put myself together. Physically, I'm there. Dressed. Heart and brain functioning at a semi-normal pattern again. But I still feel scattered all over the room. Vulnerable. A mess of craving and splintered memories.

"What now?"

He glances toward the bed. "Rest, I suppose. We should leave early."

I take his hand in mine. Unexpected relief floods me when he doesn't reject the contact.

"Lie down with me."

"I wasn't vigilant enough before and nearly got us killed. I'm not letting that happen again."

"You need to sleep too."

He threads our fingers tighter. "I'll be fine. I can keep watch until daybreak. Then we'll get out of here."

"Please," I whisper. "Just a few minutes."

He takes a deep breath and touches my face gently. "What is it about you?"

I smile, unable to ignore the little flutter of happiness his words give me.

We move together to the little bed. There's barely enough room for one, but I don't care. I make it work and use it as an excuse to tangle myself in his familiar warmth. I'm scared to death of losing the magic between us. I just want a few minutes. Then I know I'll want more.

The church is quiet, save a few concerning creaks that soon become normal sounds. Wind. Tree branches scratching the roof. I sigh and try to turn off the fear that doesn't ever seem to go away altogether now. I nuzzle against Tristan's chest and let his scent chase it away a little more.

"Tristan?"

He hums and tucks me a little closer.

"What if they don't stop looking for us?"

He's quiet for so long that tendrils of sleep begin to wrap around my thoughts before I hear him finally speak.

"They won't."

10

TRISTAN

Gunshots. They're whizzing by and dropping men to the ground all around me. They're punching into my flesh. They're killing me.

The voices shouting are a tangle of English and the Arabic I've yet to pick up. I can't make sense of anything past the panic and the agony and the instinct to get the fuck out of here as fast as I can.

But every time I get up, I stumble back down, lightheaded and dodging the bullets that are still flying, puncturing the dusty walls of this hut. I lie on my stomach while hot rays of sunlight pour through the crude window openings until the room begins to cool and all I can see is the bright white overwhelming my vision.

"Stone! Stone!"

Faces imprint in flashes on the white. Men like me. Fear and fire in their eyes. Then they're gone and my whole body is vibrating. I'm moving. Strip after strip of fluorescent lights fly by above me. I can't tell if I'm chasing the lights or running from them.

"You're going to be all right. Just stay with me. Keep your eyes open." A man in green scrubs places a clear plastic mask over my face. "Just breathe, Tristan."

I suck in a half breath that shoots pain down every limb. I try to cry out, but everything disappears, and I'm transported somewhere else.

A brushed metal table beams light into my eyes from the industrial lamp swaying above us. A woman with piercing blue eyes and red hair pulled tight from her fair-skinned face sits across from me in a blue pin-striped business suit.

"I'm Jay. I'll be your contact moving forward."

I look down at myself. I'm in street clothes. I can feel the bandages wrinkling against my skin underneath. The pain is gone, replaced by a muddy sort of consciousness. I'm pretty sure this isn't a dream, though. I think I'm alive.

"How did I get here?"

"You had some of the military's best doctors caring for you. You were put into a deep coma while you recovered."

"Is that why I feel… My head. It's like everything is cloudy."

Jay offers a tight smile. I can't tell if it's sympathetic or something else. "You will have a difficult time accessing your memory. Don't try to fight it, Tristan."

"I don't understand."

"The trauma from the mission combined with the induced coma you were in for several weeks resulted in what we call dissociative fugue. Your memory is…" She drums her fingers on her knee, averting her gaze for only a moment. "Think of it as a fresh start. For the sake of your safety and everyone involved, it's

probably for the best that things turned out this way."

I wince. "Everyone involved?"

"If it weren't for the valuable skills you demonstrated over the past few years, I'm not sure you'd be given this opportunity. Several people lost their lives. There's a lot of blood on your hands, Tristan." She's quiet for a moment. "Take this for what it is. A second chance."

I press the heels of my hands to my eyes and rub vigorously. Maybe this is a dream. Everything is so confusing. The things she's saying don't match the synapses firing in my brain. Something's off. Something's wrong. Really wrong.

"What do I do now?"

"You won't be safe in the US for a while. We've set you up with a place just outside of Rio de Janeiro. You can heal and rest there. Then I'll be in touch when we have a job for you."

"A job?"

She's silent a moment. "The second chance doesn't come without cost."

Jay's laser focus from across the table makes me uncomfortable, like she can see all the things that won't come into view for me right now.

"What do you need me to do?"

"You'll take assignments that only someone entirely off the grid can take. You'll need to take every precaution to keep yourself safe after a hit. We won't be there to support you unless we absolutely need another agent involved. You'll receive all the pertinent information, and then you'll be compensated when the work is done. No paperwork. No red tape."

My mouth is dry. I think it's the pain medication that's

making all this feel so surreal and out of reach. I take a drink from the water glass in front of me.

"Listen, I just want to go home."

Jay leans in. Her eyes are cold, like deep ocean water.

"Where's home, Tristan?"

I jerk awake. Isabel is asleep beside me. Peaceful. Damn near angelic in the wake of the nightmare. A mix of relief and gut-wrenching fear washes over me. Fear that I'll fail her—both of us—if I can't keep her safe. I rise gingerly from the bed so as not to rouse her and go to my bag. I pull out my laptop, sit at the desk, and open the protected chat. Jay's unanswered messages stare back at me.

I'm a grown man. I've killed more men than I can count, but somehow I can hardly bring myself to acknowledge or challenge her. We both know what's gone down. Soon enough she'll know even more, once someone discovers Crow and gets him out of the impossible bind I left him in.

The cursor blinks, taunting me. With no one to report back, she could believe I'm dead, but she's too smart for that.

I begin typing.

> **RED: You'll have to do better than that.**

A few minutes pass with no reply. I look out the window. Early dawn is approaching. We'll have to leave soon, before the streets come back to life. The sound of a return message draws my attention back to the screen.

JAY: You're making a mistake.

I grimace, as pissed off as ever. Three years of clean, quiet, anonymous hits, and now I'm her mark.

RED: So are you.

JAY: Bring her in and we can talk.

She knows as well as I do that will never happen. Either some part of her wants to salvage the relationship, or Isabel's death is more of a priority than I realized. My money is on the latter.

I hear a rustle outside the window. I grab my gun and steal a glance at Isabel, oblivious in her slumber.

There's a soft rap at the door. "Isabel."

I rise at the muffled sound of the priest's voice. I open the door a crack to find him standing there with a cloth-covered basket. He lifts it. "Breakfast for you."

I reach out and take it, noting the unease and exhaustion on the old man's features.

I'm ready to close the door, when he lifts his hand, stopping me. "I was awake all night watching the street. The same black truck passes back and forth every hour or so." His lips press together in a worried line. "It doesn't feel right to me."

I poke my head around the door. The street is quiet. "When's the last time you saw the car?"

"Twenty minutes."

"Did they see you?"

He shrugs. "Not many people notice an old man like me."

"We'll leave soon. Thanks for this."

He nods and waves a silent farewell. After ensuring Isabel is still sleeping, I slip outside.

I take my phone out and hesitate over Mateus's number before dialing. It rings only once.

"Tristan. Is she okay?"

"We're fine. For now."

"What's happened?"

I hesitate over my next words. "Do you remember what you said about letting things go…to get what you really want?"

He's quiet for a moment. "You're sending her home."

"I'll get her out of Petrópolis, but I'm running out of time. They're closing in." I hesitate. "Can you help me get her out of Brazil?"

"I'll do anything you ask of me, Tristan. That's not the question."

"What's the damn question, Mateus? Help me or don't."

"The question is whether you trust me to."

ISABEL

Tristan's memory might be lost, but I swear I can still see vengeance haunting his eyes where I used to see his joy. He woke me this morning quickly and quietly. Danger wasn't on our heels, but we're on the move. To where, he won't say. I pick at the moist bread Antonio brought to us as we drive from one town to the next.

"Are you upset with me?"

His brows knit firmly together. "Why would I be upset with you?"

"I don't know. Last night happened. Guys can be weird after that."

"Guys?" He shoots me a narrow look.

I huff out a sigh. "Never mind."

Silence stretches between us for a long time before he finally speaks again.

"I enjoyed last night. Doesn't change the fact that today is a new day, we're in danger, and I needed to get you out of there. Your friendly neighborhood priest was on the lookout all night. Jay's people weren't far."

"Who's Jay?"

"Former employer," he says flatly.

I lean forward, my jaw slack. "Are you kidding me? You work for the monsters who are trying to kill us?"

The muscle in his jaw ticks. "I'm a contractor. We're having a disagreement about the terms of our arrangement."

I stare in stunned disbelief. Then…suddenly…it all makes sense. The blocks of cash. The guns and willingness to use them to any end. Tristan's near-complete disregard for human life. I push his tender moments out of the picture because they cloud the view. And it's all coming into focus.

Your comrades.

Someone wants you dead.

I know the price on her head. What's mine?

A rush of enlightenment crashes over me as we make a turn down a narrow, paved road. It's leading us toward an open field and tarmac. There are a few small planes and a helicopter parked around an old hangar. A larger, sleeker jet sits at the center of the tarmac, its boarding door open with stairs leading up to it. A young man is pacing beside it, stopping as Tristan parks.

"Come on," he says.

I get out of the car as he pops the trunk. "Where are we going?"

"Not we. You."

The man comes our way, extending his hand to Tristan. "You must be Mateus's friend. I'm Leo, your pilot." He nods to me. "*Senhorita.*"

Tristan shakes his hand before grabbing my backpack and slamming the trunk shut.

"Leo's going to fly you to Panama."

"Panama?" My eyes widen.

"They'll be expecting you to try to get a flight out of Rio or São Paulo. They'll pluck you from security or God knows what else. It's too risky."

"Okay." I try to will my voice not to shake.

"You'll be able to get to Panama City in the jet without refueling. Leo will take care of customs. But this is important. As soon as you get there, you're going to buy a ticket to DC. No stops. And use cash in case they're tracking your cards. I can't risk you getting on their radar before you're in the air. Understand?"

My breathing ticks up rapidly. This is too much too fast. I can't think anything through. All I can do is trust Tristan, and he's scaring the hell out of me with this plan. I don't even like flying.

"What about you? I can't just leave you here."

"I can't protect you here. It'll be easier for you to get back home without me. They're going to be expecting both of us."

"I'm not leaving without you. I don't care what you say." I cross my arms and prepare to hold my ground. I can't leave him… I can't let him go again.

Leo's eyes widen a fraction. "Let me know when you're ready. I'll wait for you."

"She's ready," Tristan answers for me. He hands the man my backpack.

I try to grab it back, but Leo is already moving toward the plane and out of earshot. My nostrils flare. "Enough of this shit, Tristan. You need to give me answers. I've waited long enough."

"I told you. The less you know, the better."

"You mean I shouldn't know what kind of man you are?"

Tristan's jaw is tight. "What kind of man am I, Isabel?"

I hold his steady stare, uncertain if I'm actually ready for the truth. "Tell me why you came for me that day."

He steps closer, dominating my personal space. That quickly, I'm caught in a tornado of our intense sexual attraction and the inherent fear Tristan inspires at moments like these.

"You want to know the truth?" His voice is dangerously low.

Lust pulses through me at the most inopportune time.

Maybe if I kiss him, he won't have to tell me what I fear to be true. I fist my hand in his shirt. It steadies me on shaky legs and binds him to me in some small way, regardless of what he's about to say.

He touches my chin, guiding all my attention to the silvery sky reflecting in his eyes.

"Three years ago, the Tristan you knew died. Now I take jobs that only a dead man can take. Back in Rio, I was sent to kill you. I would have been paid handsomely for it. I was ready to pull the trigger, until you said my name."

"On the street?"

He shakes his head. "I was in your apartment after you turned away Kolt. You were in bed taking care of things he badly wanted to. I was so close to going through with it, but something held me back. Then you said my name, and… I just couldn't do it." He brings his hand to my face, drawing his thumb across my cheek tenderly. "Because I didn't, there's a bounty on both our heads. And if you don't get on that plane right now, they're going to finish the job I wouldn't."

The tears I've been holding back spill over. Hot, thick tears that threaten a torrent of sobs to follow. This can't be real. This can't be happening.

"You need to go now." He pulls away, steps away, looks away.

I tighten my fist in his shirt, but he's unclenching my grip. Putting distance between us. I fight him, but I know it's useless.

He tried to kill me.

He kept me alive.

He tied me to the goddamn bed.

He killed a man who would have killed me first if given the chance.

He's not my Tristan anymore.

He's a shadow.

He's indelibly imprinted on me.

In my blurred periphery, I see Leo coming closer. Time is running out. I need more time with Tristan to figure all this out.

"When will I see you again?"

He glances to Leo and back to me. "There will be someone to meet you at Dulles. An old acquaintance."

"How will I know him?"

"Trust me, you'll be able to spot him in a crowd. He'll take you to your father as soon as it's safe."

"No." I can't hide the agony wrapped around that one word.

His hardened expression softens.

"Go… Please, Isabel. Just go."

Continue The Red Ledger with

PART 2

Available Now in e-Book!

OR

REBORN
(Parts 1, 2 & 3)

Available Now in Print

ACKNOWLEDGMENTS

December 2, 2014, I woke up from a nap with an intense dream in my head. The notes I took all that time ago would eventually become the first scene of *Reborn*. To be publishing this book almost four years later is literally a dream come true!

So many people have helped me bring this first volume of Tristan and Isabel's story to the world.

To those who have given their time and thoughtful feedback to help me make this book the very best it could be—my husband and first reader Jonathan, my editor Scott Saunders, my story consultant Remi Ibraheem, and my beta readers, Cleida, Carol, Amber, Krystin, Megan, Delanea, Linda, Martha, Melissa, Lauren, Stephanie, Beatrice, Cathy, April, Jordan, Jamie, Elyn, Sue, Kika, Danielle, and Kristin... Thank you!

To my sprint ladies for giving me critical motivational pushes and support the whole way—Angel Payne, Victoria Blue, Mia Michelle... Thank you!

To Solange, my constant cheerleader for this little dream of a book... Thank you!

To everyone on the Waterhouse Press team who has taken special care of this project every little step of the way... Thank you!

To my readers and amazing Team Wild crew, you have

embraced the concept for *The Red Ledger* since the moment I decided to bring it out of hiding. Thank you for your daily support and bringing so much joy to my world as an author. I can't wait to share *Recall* with you very soon!

ABOUT THE AUTHOR

Meredith Wild is a #1 *New York Times*, *USA Today*, and international bestselling author. After publishing her debut novel, *Hardwired*, in September 2013, Wild used her ten years of experience as a tech entrepreneur to push the boundaries of her "self-published" status, becoming stocked in brick-and-mortar bookstore chains nationwide and forging relationships with major retailers.

In 2014, Wild founded her own imprint, Waterhouse Press, under which she hit #1 on the *New York Times* and *Wall Street Journal* bestseller lists. She has been featured on *CBS This Morning* and the *Today Show*, and in the *New York Times*, the *Hollywood Reporter*, *Publishers Weekly*, and the *Examiner*. Her foreign rights have been sold in twenty-two languages.